MEN WITHOUT WOMEN

ALSO BY **HARUKI MURAKAMI**

FICTION

After Dark

After the Quake

Blind Willow, Sleeping Woman

Colorless Tsukuru Tazaki and His Years of Pilgrimage

Dance Dance Dance

The Elephant Vanishes

Hard-Boiled Wonderland and the End of the World

Kafka on the Shore

Norwegian Wood

South of the Border, West of the Sun

Sputnik Sweetheart

The Strange Library

A Wild Sheep Chase

Wind/Pinball

The Wind-Up Bird Chronicle

1Q84

NONFICTION

Absolutely on Music: Conversations with Seiji Ozawa

Underground: The Tokyo Gas Attack and the Japanese Psyche

What I Talk About When I Talk About Running

HARUKI MURAKAMI

MEN WITHOUT WOMEN

STORIES

Translated from the Japanese
by Philip Gabriel and Ted Goossen

Harvill *Secker*
LONDON

1 3 5 7 9 10 8 6 4 2

Harvill Secker, an imprint of Vintage,
20 Vauxhall Bridge Road,
London SW1V 2SA

Harvill Secker is part of the Penguin Random House group of companies
whose addresses can be found at global.penguinrandomhouse.com

Penguin
Random House
UK

First published by Harvill Secker in 2017
First published in Japan as *Onna no inai Otokotachi* by
Bungei Shunjū Ltd., Tokyo, in 2014

A CIP catalogue record for this book is available from the British Library

penguin.co.uk/vintage

ISBN 9781911215370

Printed and bound in Great Britain by Clays Ltd, St Ives PLC

Some stories first appeared, in slightly different form, in the following
publications: 'Drive My Car' first appeared in *Freeman's* (October 2015);
'Kino' (Feb/Mar 2015), 'Samsa in Love' (October 2013), 'Scheherazade'
(October 2014) and 'Yesterday' (June 2014) all first appeared in *The New Yorker*.

Penguin Random House is committed to a sustainable future
for our business, our readers and our planet. This book is made
from Forest Stewardship Council® certified paper.

CONTENTS

MEN WITHOUT

WOMEN

DRIVE MY CAR

BASED ON THE MANY TIMES he had ridden in cars driven by women, Kafuku had reached the conclusion that most female drivers fell into one of two categories: either they were a little too aggressive or a little too timid. Luckily—and we should all be grateful for this—the latter were far more common. Generally speaking, women were more cautious than men behind the wheel. Of course, that caution was nothing to complain about. Yet their driving style tended to irritate others on the road.

Most of the aggressive women, on the other hand, seemed convinced they were great drivers. In most cases, they showed their timid sisters nothing but scorn, and were proud that they, at least, weren't like that. They were oblivious to the gasps and slammed brakes that accompanied their sudden and daring lane changes, and to the less-than-complimentary words directed at them by their fellow drivers.

Of course, not all women belonged to one of those two groups. There were those *normal* drivers who were neither too aggressive nor too cautious. Some could even be called experts. Nevertheless, somehow or other, even with those expert female drivers, Kafuku usually sensed a certain tension. There was no concrete reason that he could point to, but from where he sat in the passenger seat he felt a kind of friction in the air, and it made him tense. His throat would turn dry, or he would start saying foolish, totally unnecessary things just to bury the silence.

Certainly there were good and bad male drivers too. Yet in most cases their driving didn't create the same charged atmosphere. It wasn't that they were especially laid back. In reality, they were probably tense too. Nevertheless, they seemed to be able to separate their tension and who they were in a natural—likely unconscious—way. They could converse and act normally even while focused on the road. As in, *that belongs there and this belongs here.* Kafuku had no idea where this difference between men and women drivers came from.

Kafuku seldom drew distinctions between men and women in his daily life. Nor was he apt to perceive any difference in ability between the sexes. There were as many women as men in his line of work, and he actually felt more at ease working with women. For the most part, women paid closer attention to details, and they listened well. The only problem occurred when he got in a car and found a woman sitting beside him with her hands on the steering wheel. That he found impossible to ignore. Yet he had never voiced his opinion on the matter to anyone. Somehow the topic seemed inappropriate.

·　　·　　·

Thus when Oba, who ran the garage where he serviced his car, recommended a young woman to be his personal driver, Kafuku looked less than thrilled. Oba smiled at his reaction. Yeah, I know how you feel, the mechanic's face said.

"But she's one heck of a driver. I can guarantee that, no problem. Why don't you meet her and see for yourself?"

"Sure, since you recommend her," Kafuku said. He needed to hire a driver as quickly as possible, and Oba was someone he trusted. He had known the impish man with hair that bristled like wire for fifteen years. When it came to automobiles, Oba's word was as good as gold.

"To be on the safe side, I'm going to take a look at your wheel alignment, but assuming that's okay, you can pick up your car the day after tomorrow at two p.m. Why don't I ask the girl to come then too, so you can check her out, maybe have her drive you around the neighborhood? You can level with me if you don't like her. No skin off my nose if you don't."

"How old is she?"

"Never got around to asking. But I would guess in her mid-twenties," Oba said. Then he gave a slight frown. "Like I said, she's a great driver, but . . ."

"But?"

"Well, how should I put this, she's not exactly the congenial type."

"In what way?"

"She's brusque, shoots from the hip when she talks, which isn't often. And she smokes like a chimney," Oba said. "You'll see for yourself when you meet her, but she's not what you'd call cute, either. Almost never smiles, and she's a bit *homely*, to be honest."

"That's not a problem. I'd feel uncomfortable if she were too pretty, and there could be nasty rumors."

"Sounds like it might be a good match, then."

"Apart from all that, she's a good driver, right?"

"Yeah, she's solid. Not just for a woman, but as a driver, pure and simple."

"What kind of work is she doing now?"

"I'm not too sure. I think she scrapes by as a convenience store clerk, courier service driver, stuff like that. Short-term jobs she can drop right away when something better pops up. She came here on a friend's recommendation looking for work, but things are a bit tight, and I can't take on anyone full time right now. I give her a shout when I need extra help. But she's really reliable. And she never takes a drink."

Kafuku's face darkened with the mention of liquor, and his fingers unconsciously rose to his lips.

"The day after tomorrow at two it is, then," Kafuku said. Brusque, close-mouthed, not at all cute—he was intrigued.

Two days later, at two in the afternoon, the yellow Saab 900 convertible was fixed and ready to drive. The dented right front fender had been returned to its original shape, the painted patch blending almost perfectly with the rest of the car. The engine was tuned, the transmission readjusted, and new brake pads and wiper blades installed. The car was freshly washed, its tires polished, its body waxed. As always, Oba's work was flawless. Kafuku had owned the car for twelve years and put nearly a hundred thousand miles on it. The canvas roof was showing its age. When it poured he had to worry about leaks. But for the time being, Kafuku had no intention of buying a newer vehicle. Not only had the Saab never given him any major trouble, he was personally attached to it. He loved driving with the top down, regardless of the season. In the winter, he wore a thick coat and wrapped a scarf around his neck, while in the summer he donned dark sunglasses and a cap. He would drive around the city, shifting gears with great pleasure and looking up to take in passing clouds and birds perched on electric wires whenever he stopped at a traffic light. Those moments had been a key part of his life for many years. Kafuku walked slowly around his car, inspecting it closely like a horse before a race.

His wife had still been alive when he had purchased it new. She had chosen the yellow color. During the first few years, they had often gone out for drives together. Since his wife didn't have a license, Kafuku had always been the one behind the wheel. They had taken a number of road trips as well, to places like Izu, Hakone, and Nasu. Yet, for what was now nearly ten years, he had always driven alone. He had seen several women since his wife's death, but none had ever sat beside him in the passenger seat. For some reason, the opportunity had never arisen. Nor had he ever taken the car outside the city, apart from those times when work made it necessary.

"There's some inevitable wear and tear, but she's in good shape," Oba said, running his palm over the dashboard, as if stroking the neck of a large dog. "Totally reliable. Swedish cars of this age are built to last. You have to keep your eye on the electrical system, but they're fundamentally sound. And I've been looking after this baby really well."

While Kafuku was signing the necessary papers and

going over the itemized bill, the young woman showed up. She was about five foot five, not at all fat but broad-shouldered and powerfully built. There was an oval-shaped, purple birthmark to the right of the nape of her neck that she seemed to have no qualms exposing. Her thick jet-black hair was fastened at the back, to keep it out of her way. No matter how you looked at her she was hardly a beauty, and there was something off-putting about her face, as Oba had suggested. The remnants of teenage acne dotted her cheeks. She had big, strikingly clear eyes that looked out suspiciously on the world, their dark brown irises all the more striking because of their size. Her large, protruding ears were like satellite dishes placed in some remote landscape. She was wearing a man's herringbone jacket that was a bit too heavy for May, brown cotton pants, and a pair of black Converse sneakers. Beneath the white long-sleeved T-shirt under her jacket Kafuku could see her larger-than-average breasts.

Oba introduced her to Kafuku. Her name was Watari. Misaki Watari.

"There are no kanji for Misaki—it's written in hiragana," she said. "If you need a résumé I can get you one." Kafuku detected a note of defiance in her voice.

"No need for a résumé at this stage," he said, shaking his head. "You can handle a manual shift, correct?"

"I prefer manual," she said in an icy tone. She sounded like a staunch vegetarian who had just been asked if she ate lettuce.

"It's an old car, so there's no GPS."

"I don't need it. I worked as a courier for a while. I've got a map of the city in my head."

"Why don't we take a little test drive? The weather's good so we can put the top down."

"Where would you like to go?"

Kafuku thought for a moment. They were not far from Shinohashi.

"Take a right at the Tengenji intersection and then drive to the underground parking lot at the Meijiya supermarket, so I can do a bit of shopping. After that we'll head up the slope to Arisugawa Park, and then down past the French embassy and onto Gaien Nishi Dori. Then we'll swing back here."

"Got it," she said. She asked for no further details about the route. Taking the key from Oba, she quickly adjusted the driver's seat and the mirrors. It appeared she already knew where all the buttons and levers were located. She stepped on the clutch and tested the gears. Then she pulled a pair of green Ray-Ban sunglasses from the pocket of her jacket and put them on. She turned and nodded to Kafuku to signal she was ready to go.

"A cassette player," she said as if to herself, glancing at the audio system.

"I like cassettes," Kafuku said. "They're easier than CDs. I use them to rehearse my lines."

"Haven't seen one of those for a while."

"When I started driving they were all eight-track players," Kafuku said.

Misaki didn't reply, but her expression suggested eight-track players were something new to her.

As Oba had guaranteed, she was an excellent driver. She operated the car smoothly, with no sudden jerks. The road was crowded, with frequent stoplights, but she was focused on changing gears smoothly. The movement of her eyes told him that. When he closed his own eyes, though, he found it next to impossible to tell when she shifted. Only the sound of the engine let him know which gear the car was in. The touch of her foot on the brake and accelerator pedals was light and careful. Best of all, she was entirely relaxed. In fact, she seemed more at ease when driving. Her blunt, impersonal expression became softer, and her eyes gentler. Yet she was every bit as taciturn. She would answer his questions and nothing more.

The absence of conversation didn't bother Kafuku. He wasn't good at small talk. While he didn't dislike talking to people he knew well about things that mattered, he otherwise preferred to remain silent. He sat back in the passenger seat and idly watched the city streets go by. After years behind the wheel, the view from where he now sat seemed fresh and new.

He had her parallel park several times on busy Gaien Nishi Dori, a test she passed easily with a minimum of wasted effort. She had a good feel for the car, and her timing was perfect. She smoked only when they were stopped at traffic lights. Marlboros seemed her brand of choice. The moment the light changed she snuffed out the cigarette. Her butts had no lipstick on them. Nor were her fingernails polished or manicured. She seemed to wear virtually no makeup.

"Mind if I ask you a few questions?" Kafuku said when they were approaching Arisugawa Park.

"Go right ahead."

"Where did you learn to drive?"

"I grew up in Hokkaido, in the mountains. I started driving in my early teens. You have to have a car in a place like that. The roads are icy almost half the year. You can't avoid becoming a good driver."

"But you don't learn how to parallel park in the mountains, do you?"

She didn't answer that. Doubtless she found the question not worth bothering with.

"Did Oba explain to you why I need a driver all of a sudden?"

Misaki answered in a flat, emotionless voice, her eyes trained on the traffic ahead. "You're an actor, and you're on stage six days a week at the moment. You have always driven to the theater. You don't like taxis or taking the subway. That's because you rehearse your lines on the way. Not long ago you had a minor accident and your license was suspended. Because you'd been drinking a little, and there was a problem with your eyesight."

Kafuku nodded. It felt as if someone were describing her dream to him.

"The eye exam the police required turned up a trace of glaucoma. It appears I have a blind spot. On the right side, in the corner. I had no idea."

The amount of alcohol involved was negligible, so they had been able to hush it up. No one had leaked it to the media. But theater management couldn't ignore the problem with his eyesight. As things stood, a car might approach him from behind on his right side, and he would miss seeing it. Management thus insisted that he stop driving, at least until tests showed the problem had been fixed.

"Mr. Kafuku?" Misaki asked. "Is it all right if I call you that? It's not a stage name?"

"It's an unusual name, but it's really mine," Kafuku

said. "The kanji mean 'House of Good Fortune.' Sounds auspicious, but there hasn't been any payoff as far as I can see. None of my relatives are what you could call wealthy."

After a period of silence, Kafuku told her the chauffeur's salary. Not a lot of money. But it was all his theater could afford. Although his name was well known, he wasn't famous like TV and movie stars, and there was a limit to how much money could be made on the stage. For an actor of his class, hiring a personal driver, even if only for a few months, was an exceptional luxury.

"Your work schedule will be subject to change, but these days my life is centered around the theater, which means your mornings are basically free. You can sleep till noon if you wish. I'll make sure you can quit by eleven at night—if I have to work later than that I'll take a taxi home. You will have one day off every week."

"I accept," Misaki said simply.

"The work shouldn't be that taxing. The hard part will be waiting around for hours with nothing to do."

Misaki did not respond. Her lips were set in a straight line. The look on her face said that she had tackled far more difficult jobs.

"I don't mind if you smoke while the top is down," Kafuku said. "But please don't when it's up."

"Agreed."

"Do you have any conditions?"

"Nothing in particular." She narrowed her eyes as she carefully downshifted. "I like the car," she added.

They drove the rest of the way without talking. When they arrived back at the garage, Kafuku called Oba over to give him the news. "I've decided to hire her," he announced.

Misaki started working as Kafuku's personal driver the next day. She would arrive at his Ebisu apartment building at half past three in the afternoon, take the yellow Saab from the underground garage, and drive him to a theater in Ginza. They drove with the top down unless it was raining. Kafuku practiced his lines on the way, reciting with the cassette recording. The play was a Meiji-era adaptation of Chekhov's *Uncle Vanya*. He played the role of Uncle Vanya. He knew the lines by heart, but ran through them anyway to calm his nerves before a performance. This was his long-standing habit.

As a rule, they listened to Beethoven string quartets on the way home. Kafuku never tired of them—he found them perfectly suited to thinking or, if he preferred, thinking about nothing at all. If he wanted something lighter, he chose classic American rock. Groups like the Beach Boys, the Rascals, CCR, the Temptations, and so on. The popular music of his youth. Misaki never commented on his selection. He couldn't tell if his music pleased or pained her, or if she was listening at all, for that matter. She was a young woman who didn't show her emotions.

Under normal circumstances, Kafuku found reciting his lines in the presence of others stressful, but those inhibitions vanished with Misaki. In that sense, he appreciated her lack of expressiveness and her cool, distant personality. He might roar beside her while he rehearsed, but she acted as though she heard nothing. Indeed it was quite possible that her attention was solely focused on the road. Perhaps driving put her in a Zen-like frame of mind.

Kafuku had no idea what Misaki thought of him as a person. Was she kindly disposed, or unimpressed and disinterested, or did she loathe him and put up with him just to keep her job? He was in the dark. But it didn't matter to him all that much how she felt. He liked her smooth and assured driving, her lack of chatter, and the way she kept her feelings to herself.

After the night's performance ended, Kafuku washed off his stage makeup, changed his clothes, and left the theater as quickly as possible. He didn't like dawdling. He knew almost none of his fellow actors. He would call Misaki on his cell phone and have her drive to the stage door to pick him up. When he stepped outside, the yellow Saab would be waiting for him. By the time he got back to his Ebisu apartment, it would be a little after ten thirty. This pattern repeated itself on a nightly basis.

He had other work as well. He spent one day a week shooting a drama series at a TV studio in the middle of the city. It was your garden-variety detective show, but the audience was large and it paid well. He played a fortune-teller who assisted the female lead detective. To prepare for the role, he had dressed in fortune-teller's garb and set up a booth on the street, where he told the fortunes of a number of passersby. Word had it that many of his prognostications had hit the mark. When his day of shooting ended he went straight from the studio to the theater in Ginza. That was the risky part. On weekends, after the matinee, he would teach a night class at an acting school. He loved working with young actors. Misaki ferried him around for all these activities. She drove him from place to place without the slightest fuss, always on time, so that Kafuku grew used to sitting beside her in the Saab's passenger seat. On occasion, he even fell fast asleep.

When the weather grew warmer, Misaki replaced her herringbone jacket with a lighter summer jacket. She always wore a jacket while working. Probably it was her equivalent of a chauffeur's uniform. With the rainy season, the roof remained up more frequently.

Sitting there in the passenger seat, Kafuku often thought of his dead wife. For some reason, he recalled her more frequently now that Misaki was doing the driving. His wife had been an actor too, a stunning woman two years his junior. Kafuku was what was generally known as a character actor, hired to play supporting roles that were quirky in some way or other. He had a long and narrow face, and had begun to grow bald while he was still quite young. Not the leading-man type. His beautiful wife, on the other hand, was a real leading lady, and her roles and income reflected that status. As they got older, however, he became known as a skilled actor with a distinctive persona, while her star began to wane. But they both respected the other's work, and so the shifts in their popularity and income never caused problems.

Kafuku adored his wife. He had fallen deeply in love with her when they first met (he was twenty-nine), and this feeling had remained unchanged until the day she died (he had been forty-nine then). He hadn't slept with another woman in all their years of marriage. The urge had never arisen, although he had received his fair share of opportunities.

His wife, however, slept with other men on occasion. As far as he knew, there had been four such affairs. In other words, there were four men who had shared her bed for periods of time. She had never breathed a word to him, of course, but still it hadn't taken him long to figure out that she was sleeping with some other man in some other place. Kafuku had a sixth sense about such things, and his love for her made it impossible for him to ignore the signs, however much he would have liked to. It was easy to tell who her lovers were from the way she talked about them. Invariably, they were fellow actors working on the same film. Most were younger. The relationship would continue for the few months they were shooting the movie and die a natural death when the filming stopped. The same thing had happened four times, always following the same pattern.

Kafuku hadn't understood why she felt the need to sleep with other men. And he still didn't. Their relationship as a married couple and as life partners had been excellent from the beginning. When time permitted, they talked with passion and honesty about a wide variety of subjects, and tried to trust one another. He had thought they were a most compatible pair, both spiritually and sexually. Others in their circle also regarded them as an ideal match.

He regretted that he had not summoned his resolve while she was still alive to question her about her affairs. It was a regret that visited him frequently. He had been oh-so-close to asking her. He would have said, What were you looking for in those other men? What did you find lacking in me? But it had been mere months before the end, and she was suffering terribly as she struggled against her approaching death. He didn't have the heart to demand an answer. Then, without a word of explanation, she had vanished from Kafuku's world. The question never ventured, the answer never proffered. He was lost in those thoughts at the crematorium as he plucked her bones from the ashes. So lost that when someone whispered in his ear, Kafuku did not hear him.

Needless to say, picturing his wife in the arms of another man was painful for Kafuku. It could be no other way. When he closed his eyes, the details of their love-making would rise unbidden and then fade away, only to rise again. He didn't want to imagine such things, but he couldn't help it. The images whittled away at him like a sharp knife, steady and unrelenting. There were times he thought it would have been far better to never have known. Yet he continued to return to his core principle: that, in every situation, knowledge was better than igno-rance. However agonizing, it was necessary to confront the facts. Only through knowing could a person become strong.

The most excruciating thing, though, had been main-taining a normal life knowing his partner's secret—the effort it required to keep her in the dark. Smiling calmly when his heart was torn and his insides were bleeding. Behaving as if everything was fine while the two of them took care of the daily chores, chatted, made love at night. This was not something that a normal person could pull off. But Kafuku was a professional actor. Shedding his self, his flesh and blood, in order to inhabit a role was his calling. And he embraced this one with all his might. A role performed without an audience.

Yet if you put these things aside—excluded, in other words, the fact that she conducted occasional affairs with other men—their married life was calm and contented. Their careers proceeded smoothly, and they had no financial worries. Over the course of their nearly twenty years together, they made love countless times; for him, at least, the sex had been entirely satisfying. After she contracted uterine cancer and, in what seemed a mere instant later, passed away, he had been lucky enough to meet several women who, in the natural course of things, he had taken to bed. Yet he never experienced the same intimate joy with them that he had with his wife. All he felt was a mild sense of déjà vu, as if he were reenacting a scene from his past.

His management office needed specific information to process Misaki's paychecks, so Kafuku had to ask her to provide her address, the location of her family register, her birth date, and her driver's license number. She was living in an apartment in downtown Akabane, her family register was in Junitakicho on the island of Hokkaido, and she had just turned twenty-four. Kafuku had no idea where Junitakicho was in Hokkaido. But the fact that she was twenty-four grabbed his attention.

Kafuku's wife had given birth to a baby who had lived only three days. It was a girl. She died on her third night in the hospital nursery. Her heart stopped without warning. When they found her the next morning, she was already cold. The hospital said that she had been born with a defective heart. There had been no way to verify their story. Nor would finding the true cause of death have restored her to life. For better or for worse, they had not yet given her a name. Had she lived, she would have been twenty-four years old. Kafuku always marked the birthday of this nameless child by joining his hands in prayer. Then he would think about how old she would have been.

As one would expect, the sudden death of their child

wounded Kafuku and his wife, suspending them in a dark, heavy void. It took them a very long time to get back on their feet. They secluded themselves in their apartment, where for much of the time they lived in virtual silence. Words, they felt, could only cheapen the emotions they were feeling. She took to drinking immoderate amounts of wine. He, for a time, became a passionate, almost fanatical practitioner of calligraphy. It was as if he felt that the black symbols flowing from his brush onto the pure white paper could somehow lay bare the workings of his heart.

Nevertheless, by supporting each other, slowly but surely, the two of them recovered from their wounds enough to pass through that dangerous period. Their focus on work became even more intense. When they took on new roles, they immersed themselves totally, voraciously. She told him that she had no further desire for children, and he agreed. They would make sure she never got pregnant again. He was happy to do whatever she wanted.

Thinking back, he realized that it was at that time that her love affairs began. Perhaps the loss of their child had reawakened her sexual desire. But that was pure conjecture on his part. Nothing more than another "perhaps."

"Can I ask you something?" Misaki said.

Kafuku had been looking out the window at the passing scenery, lost in thought. He turned to her in surprise. They had been driving around together for two months, and rarely had she initiated a conversation.

"Of course," Kafuku said.

"Why did you become an actor?"

"A college friend of mine, a girl, asked me to join her theater club. I'd never been interested in acting. I wanted to play baseball. I'd been the starting shortstop on my high school team, and was pretty confident of my defensive ability. But I wasn't quite good enough for our college team. So I figured, what the heck, I might as well take a stab at something new. I wanted to spend more time with that girl, too. After I'd been acting for a while, though, it dawned on me that I really liked it. Performing allowed me to be someone other than myself. And I could revert back when the performance ended. I really loved that."

"You loved being someone other than yourself?"

"Yes, as long as I knew I could go back."

"Did you ever not want to go back?"

Kafuku thought for a moment. No one had asked him that before. They were heading for the Takebashi exit on the Tokyo Metropolitan Expressway, and the road was jammed.

"There's no other place to go back to, is there?" Kafuku said.

Misaki didn't venture an opinion.

They were silent for a while. Kafuku removed his baseball cap, inspected its shape, and stuck it back on his head. Next to them was a tractor trailer with too many wheels to count, a huge rig that made their yellow Saab convertible feel transitory, ephemeral. Like a tiny sightseeing boat floating next to an oil tanker.

"This may be out of line," Misaki said, "but it's been on my mind. Is it okay if I ask?"

"Shoot," Kafuku said.

"Why don't you have any friends?"

Kafuku looked questioningly at Misaki's profile. "How do you know I don't have any?"

Misaki shrugged. "I've been driving you around for two months now, so I guess I can figure out that much."

Kafuku studied the tractor trailer's enormous tires for a long moment. "There haven't been many people I could call true friends," he finally said. "I wonder why."

"Even when you were a child?"

"No, I had lots of pals back then. But once I grew up I no longer felt the need for them. Especially after I got married."

"Having a wife meant you no longer needed friends?"

"I guess so. She and I were great pals too, after all."

"How old were you when you got married?"

"Thirty. We were in the same movie. She had a major supporting role, and I had a bit part."

The car inched its way forward through the traffic jam. The roof was closed, as it always was when they drove on the expressway.

"You don't drink at all?" Kafuku changed the subject.

"My body can't handle alcohol," Misaki said. "And my mother was a problem drinker, which may have something to do with it."

"Does her drinking still cause problems?"

Misaki shook her head from side to side. "My mother's dead. She was driving drunk, lost control of the steering wheel, went into a spin, and flew off the road and into a tree. She died almost instantly. I was seventeen."

"Poor woman," Kafuku said.

"What goes around comes around," Misaki said without emotion. "It was bound to happen sooner or later. The only question was when."

They were silent for a while.

"And your father?"

"I don't know where he is. He left home when I was eight and I haven't seen him since. Haven't heard from him, either. Mother always blamed me for his leaving."

"Why?"

"I was their only child. If I'd been prettier, Father never would have left. That's what Mother always said. It's because I was born ugly that he abandoned us."

"You're not ugly," Kafuku said quietly. "Your mother just preferred to think of it that way."

Misaki gave a slight shrug. "Normally she wasn't like that, but when she was drinking, she just went on and on. Repeated the same stuff over and over again. It hurt me. It's bad, I know, but I was relieved when she died."

This time the silence was even longer.

"Do you have friends?" Kafuku inquired.

Misaki shook her head. "Not a single one."

"Why?"

She didn't answer. With her eyes narrowed, she focused on the road.

Kafuku tried to take a nap, but sleep wouldn't come. The car edged forward and stopped, edged forward and stopped, as Misaki deftly shifted gears. In the adjacent lane, the tractor trailer moved ahead and fell behind, like the shadow cast by some enormous fate.

Kafuku gave up trying to sleep. "The last time I became friends with someone was nearly ten years ago," he said, opening his eyes. "Perhaps 'someone like a friend' would be more accurate. He was six or seven years younger than me, a heck of a nice guy. He liked to drink, so we drank and talked about all kinds of things."

Misaki nodded and waited for him to continue. Kafuku hesitated for a moment before plunging in.

"To tell you the truth, he was one of my wife's lovers. He didn't know that I knew, though."

It took Misaki a long moment to get her head around what she had just heard. "You mean he was having sex with your wife?" she said at last.

"That's right. I think he was having sex with my wife on a regular basis for three or four months."

"How did you know?"

"She hid it from me, of course, but I could tell. It would take too long to explain how. But there was no question. My imagination wasn't playing tricks on me."

When they stopped for a moment, Misaki reached up with both hands to adjust the rearview mirror. "Didn't that get in the way of your friendship?"

"Quite the opposite," Kafuku said. "I made him my friend precisely because he had slept with my wife."

Misaki didn't say anything. She waited for him to go on.

"How can I put this . . . I wanted to understand. Why she slept with him, why he was the one she wanted. At least that was my motive in the beginning."

Misaki took a long, deep breath. Her chest rose beneath her jacket, then sank back. "But wasn't that awfully painful? Drinking and talking with a man you knew had slept with your wife?"

"It wasn't easy," Kafuku said. "It made me think things I would prefer to have ignored. Remember things I would rather have forgotten. But I was acting. That is my profession, after all."

"Becoming somebody different," Misaki said.

"That's right."

"And then going back to who you are."

"That's right," Kafuku said. "Whether you want to or not. But the place you return to is always slightly different from the place you left. That's the rule. It can never be exactly the same."

A fine rain began to fall. Misaki turned on the wipers. "So then did you figure it out? Why your wife slept with him?"

"No." Kafuku said, shaking his head. "I never understood. He had some qualities that I lacked. All right, *a lot* of qualities, I guess. But I could never figure out which of those had caught her fancy. Our actions aren't based on specifics like that—we can't pinpoint why we do what we do. Relationships between people, especially between men and women, operate on—what should I say—a more general level. More vague, more self-centered, more pathetic."

Misaki thought for a moment. "But still," she said, "you stayed friends with him even though you didn't understand, right?"

Kafuku took off his baseball cap again and placed it on his lap. "It's hard to explain," he said, rubbing the top of his head with his palm. "Once you really get into a role, it's hard to find the right moment to stop. No matter how it preys on your emotions, you have to go with the flow until the performance has taken its shape, the point where its true meaning becomes clear. It's the same with music. A song doesn't reach a proper end until it arrives at a final, predetermined chord. Do you understand what I mean?"

Misaki drew a Marlboro from her pack and placed it

between her lips. But she never smoked when the top was up, and it stayed unlit.

"So was the guy still sleeping with your wife when you were friends?"

"No, he wasn't," said Kafuku. "If he had been, it would have made things, how should I say . . . too complicated. We became friends not long after my wife's death."

"So were you *real* friends? Or was it all just acting?"

Kafuku thought for a while. "It was both. It's gotten so I have a hard time drawing a clear line between the two. In the end, that's what serious acting is all about."

From the beginning, Kafuku had been able to feel something approaching affection for the man. His name was Takatsuki, and he was a tall, good-looking fellow, the classic romantic lead. He was in his early forties and not an especially skilled actor. Nor did he have what one could call a distinctive presence. His range of roles was limited. As a general rule, he played nice guys, although sometimes a touch of melancholy would cloud his otherwise cheerful profile. He had a loyal following among middle-aged women. Kafuku bumped into him on occasion in the green room at the TV studio. Some six months after his wife's death, Takatsuki came up to introduce himself and express his condolences. "Your wife and I were in a film together once. I owed her a lot," Takatsuki said humbly. Kafuku thanked him. As far as he knew at that point, chronologically speaking, this man was the last of his wife's string of lovers. It was soon after the end of their affair that his wife had gone to the hospital for tests and been diagnosed with advanced uterine cancer.

"Forgive me, but I'd like to ask a favor," Kafuku said when the formalities had concluded. This was his chance to broach what he had in mind.

"Is there something I can do?"

"If it's all right with you, I'd like you to grant me some of your time. To talk about my wife. Maybe have a few drinks and remember her together. She often spoke of you."

Takatsuki looked surprised. Perhaps shocked would be more accurate. His immaculate eyebrows inched together as he cautiously studied Kafuku's face. He seemed to be trying to discern what, if anything, might lie behind the invitation. But he could read no intent in the older man's expression. All he saw was the kind of stillness you might expect from someone who had recently lost his wife of many years. Like the surface of a pond after the ripples had spread and gone.

"I was only hoping to talk about my wife with someone who knew her," Kafuku added. "To tell the truth, it can get kind of rough when I'm sitting at home all by myself. I know it's an imposition on you, though."

Takatsuki looked relieved. His relationship with the man's wife did not seem to be under suspicion.

"It's no imposition at all. I'd be happy to make time for something like that. I just hope I won't bore you." A faint smile rose to his lips as he said these words, and the corners of his eyes crinkled with compassion. An altogether charming expression. If I were a middle-aged woman, thought Kafuku, my cheeks would be turning pink right now.

Takatsuki mentally flipped through the schedule he kept in his head. "I think I have plenty of time tomorrow night. Do you have other plans?"

Kafuku replied that he was also free then. He was

struck by how easy it was to read Takatsuki's emotions. The man was transparent—if he looked into his eyes long enough, Kafuku thought, he could probably see the wall behind him. There was nothing warped, nothing nasty. Hardly the type to dig a deep hole at night and wait for someone to fall in. But neither, in all likelihood, was he a man destined to achieve greatness as an actor.

"Where shall we meet?" asked Takatsuki.

"I leave it to you," Kafuku said. "Tell me a place, and I'll be there."

Takatsuki named a well-known bar in Ginza. He would reserve a booth, he said, so that they could talk frankly without having to worry about being overheard. Kafuku knew the spot. They shook hands goodbye. Takatsuki's hand was soft, with long slender fingers. His palm was warm and slightly damp, as if he had been sweating. Perhaps he was nervous.

After he left, Kafuku sat down on a chair in the green room, opened his right hand, and stared hard at his palm. The sensation left by the handshake was still fresh. *That hand*, those fingers, had caressed his wife's naked body. Slowly and deliberately, exploring every nook and cranny. He closed his eyes and breathed deeply. What in heaven's name was he trying to do? He felt that whatever "it" was, he had no choice but to go ahead and do it.

As he sipped single malt whiskey in the booth at the bar, Kafuku came to one conclusion. Takatsuki was still deeply attached to his wife. He had not yet grasped the immutable fact of her death, that the flesh he had known had become a pile of charred bone and ash. Kafuku could understand the way he felt. When Takatsuki's eyes grew misty recalling her, he wanted to reach out to console him. The man was quite incapable of hiding his emotions. Kafuku sensed that he could trip him up with a trick question if he so chose, induce him to confess everything.

Judging from the way Takatsuki spoke, Kafuku's wife had been the one to call a halt to their affair. "It's best we not meet anymore," was probably how she had put it. And she had followed through on her words. A relationship of several months brought to a sudden close. Nothing long and drawn out. As far as Kafuku knew, that was the pattern of all her amours (if they could be called that). But it seemed that Takatsuki couldn't handle such a quick and casual break. He must have been hoping for a more permanent bond.

Takatsuki had tried to visit her during the final phase of her cancer, but had been flatly refused. After she was admitted to the city hospital, she saw almost no one. Other than hospital staff, only three people were permitted in her room: her mother, her sister, and Kafuku. Takatsuki seemed filled with regret that he had not been able to see her during that time. He had not even known she had cancer until a few weeks before her death. The news had hit him like a thunderbolt, and still hadn't entirely sunk in. Kafuku could relate to that. Yet their feelings were far from identical. Kafuku had watched his wife waste away day by day as the end drew near, and had plucked her pure-white bones from the ashes at the crematorium. He had passed through all the stages. That made a huge difference.

As they reminisced about his wife, it hit Kafuku that he was the one doing most of the consoling. How would his wife feel if she observed them sitting together like this? The idea aroused a strange emotion in Kafuku. But he doubted the dead could think or feel anything. In his opinion, that was one of the great things about dying.

One other thing was becoming clear. Takatsuki drank way too much. There were many heavy drinkers in Kafuku's line of work—why were actors so susceptible to alcohol?—so he could tell Takatsuki's drinking was not the healthy, wholesome kind. In Kafuku's considered opinion, there were two types of drinkers: those who drank to enhance their personalities, and those who sought to rid themselves of something. Takatsuki clearly belonged to the latter group.

Kafuku could not tell what it was he was trying to get rid of. Maybe weakness in his character, or trauma from his past. Or perhaps something in the present was causing his problem. Or maybe a combination of all those things. Whatever it was, he was trying like mad either to forget it or to numb the pain it caused, which made it necessary to drink. For every drink Kafuku took, Takatsuki downed two and a half. Quite a pace.

Then again, he might have just been tense. He was, after all, sitting face-to-face with the husband of the woman with whom he had been secretly having an affair. That was bound to put him on edge. But Kafuku guessed there was more to it. A man like Takatsuki could probably only drink this way.

Kafuku drank at a careful, steady rate while keeping a close eye on his companion. When the number of glasses mounted and the younger man began to relax, Kafuku asked him if he was married. I've been married ten years and have a seven-year-old son, Takatsuki answered. Due to certain circumstances, however, he and his wife had been living apart since the previous year. A divorce was likely, and the question of who would get custody of the child loomed large. What he wanted to avoid at any cost was being unable to visit his son freely. He needed the boy in his life. He showed Kafuku his child's photograph. A handsome, sweet-looking kid.

Like most habitual drinkers, the more alcohol Takatsuki drank the more loose-lipped he became. He volunteered information he shouldn't have without being asked. Kafuku took on the role of listener, interjecting an encouraging word here and there to keep his companion talking and offering carefully selected words of comfort when consolation seemed appropriate. All the while he was amassing as much information as he could. Kafuku acted as though he had only the warmest feelings for Takatsuki. This was not a hard thing to do. He was a born listener, and he did *truly* like the younger man. In addition, the two of them had one big thing in common: both were still in love with the same beautiful, dead woman. Despite the differences in their relationships with her, neither man had been able to get over that loss. They had a lot to talk about.

"Why don't we meet again?" Kafuku suggested when the evening was winding down. "It was a pleasure talking with you. I haven't felt this good for a long time." Kafuku had taken care of the bar tab in advance. It seemed not to have dawned on Takatsuki that someone would have to pay. Alcohol led him to forget a lot of things. Some were doubtless very important.

"Certainly," Takatsuki said, looking up from his glass. "I'd love to get together again. Talking to you has taken a weight off my chest."

"I feel that our meeting was somehow preordained," Kafuku said. "Perhaps my late wife brought us together."

There was some truth to that.

They exchanged cell phone numbers. Then they shook hands and parted.

Thus the two men became friends. Drinking buddies, to be more accurate. They would get in touch, meet at a bar, and talk about a variety of subjects. Not once did they share a meal. Bars were their only venue. Kafuku had never seen Takatsuki eat anything more substantial than a light snack to accompany his liquor. For all he knew, the guy might never eat solid food. Except for the occasional beer, the only drink he ever ordered was whiskey. Single malt was his preference.

Their topics varied, but at some point the conversation would always return to Kafuku's dead wife. Kafuku told stories from her younger days while Takatsuki listened intently. He looked like a researcher probing a key subject's memory to assemble a comprehensive database about someone else. Kafuku found himself enjoying those moments.

One night, the two were drinking in Aoyama at a small, nondescript bar tucked away on a narrow lane behind the Nezu Museum. The bartender was a quiet man of about forty, and a skinny gray cat was curled up on a display shelf in a corner of the room. It appeared to be an alley cat that had moved in for the time being. An old jazz record was spinning on the turntable. Both men liked the feel of the place, and had gone there several times before. For some reason, it often rained on the nights they met, and this night was no exception—a thin drizzle was falling outside.

"She was a wonderful woman," Takatsuki said, study-ing his hands on the table. They were attractive hands for a man already in middle age. There were no wrinkles around his eyes, either, and his fingernails were tended with care. "You were fortunate to find her, Mr. Kafuku, and to have shared a life together."

"You're right," Kafuku said. "I guess I was happy then. But that much happiness can lead to an equal amount of pain."

"In what way?"

Kafuku picked up his glass and swirled the chunk of ice in it. "I worried that I might lose her. Just imagining that made my heart ache."

"I know that feeling," Takatsuki said.

"How so?"

"I mean . . . ," Takatsuki said, groping for the right words. "Losing someone that wonderful."

"In general."

"Yes," Takatsuki said. He nodded several times, as if trying to convince himself. "I can only imagine what it must be like."

Kafuku fell silent. He let the silence linger as long as possible. At last he spoke.

"In the end, though, I lost her. Gradually, in the beginning, then completely. Like something that is eroded bit by bit. The process began slowly until finally a tidal wave swept it all away, the roots and everything . . . Understand what I mean?"

"I think I do."

Like hell you do, Kafuku said in his heart.

"Here's what hurts the most," Kafuku said. "I didn't *truly* understand her—or at least some crucial part of her. And it may well end that way now that she's dead and gone. Like a small, locked safe lying at the bottom of the ocean. It hurts a lot."

Takatsuki thought for a moment before speaking.

"But, Mr. Kafuku, can any of us ever perfectly understand another person? However much we may love them?"

"We lived together for nearly twenty years," Kafuku said. "As man and wife, but also as trusted friends. We were able to talk frankly about anything and everything, or so I thought. But maybe it wasn't really like that. Perhaps—how should I put this?—I had what amounted to a fatal blind spot."

"Blind spot," Takatsuki echoed.

"There was something inside her, something important, that I must have missed. If I saw it, perhaps I failed to recognize it for what it really was."

Takatsuki chewed his lip for a minute. He drained his glass and called over to the bartender to bring him another drink.

"I know what you mean," he said.

Kafuku stared hard at him. Takatsuki met his gaze for a few seconds and then looked away.

"In what sense do you know?" Kafuku said in a low voice.

The bartender brought a fresh glass of whiskey on ice and replaced Takatsuki's wet coaster with a new one. They remained silent until he had left.

"In what sense do you know?" Kafuku repeated.

Takatsuki pondered this question for a moment. Kafuku glimpsed movement in his eyes. He's wavering, he concluded. Battling the urge to reveal something. In the end, though, Takatsuki managed to calm whatever had shaken him.

"I don't think we can ever understand all that a woman

is thinking," he said. "That's what I wanted to say. No matter who that woman may be. So I doubt the blind spot you speak of is yours alone. If that's what you wish to call it, then we men are all living with the same sort of blind spot. So I don't think you should blame yourself."

"All the same, you're speaking in generalities," Kafuku said, after some thought.

"That's true," said Takatsuki.

"But I'm talking about my dead wife and me. I don't want to jump to general principles so easily."

"From what I can gather," Takatsuki said after a long silence, "your wife was a wonderful woman. I am convinced of that even as I realize my knowledge of her is no more than a hundredth of yours. If nothing else, you should feel grateful for having been able to spend twenty years of your life with such a person. But the proposition that we can look into another person's heart with perfect clarity strikes me as a fool's game. I don't care how well we think we should understand them, or how much we love them. All it can do is cause us pain. Examining your own heart, however, is another matter. I think it's possible to see what's in there if you work hard enough at it. So in the end maybe that's the challenge: to look inside your own heart as perceptively and seriously as you can, and to make peace with what you find there. If we hope to *truly* see another person, we have to start by looking within ourselves."

Takatsuki's speech seemed to have emerged from deep within him. A hidden door had swung open, if only temporarily. His words were clear and charged with conviction. He wasn't acting, that was for sure. His acting chops weren't that good. Kafuku said nothing, just looked straight into his eyes. This time Takatsuki met his gaze and held it for a long time. They could see a certain sparkle of recognition in each other's eyes.

They shook hands once again on parting. A fine rain was falling outside. After Takatsuki had walked off into the drizzle in his beige raincoat, Kafuku, as was his habit, looked down at his right palm. It was *that hand* that had caressed my wife's naked body, he thought.

Yet on this day, that thought did not suffocate him. Instead, his reaction was, yes, such things do happen. They do happen. After all, it's just a matter of flesh and blood. No more than a pile of bone and ash in the end, right? There has to be something more important than that.

If that's what you wish to call it, then we men are all living with the same sort of blind spot. The words rang in his ear for a very long time.

"So did the friendship last?" Misaki asked, her eyes fixed on the line of cars in front of them.

"It continued for about six months, give or take. We'd get together at a bar every two weeks or so and drink together," Kafuku said. "Then it ended. I ignored his phone calls. Made no attempt to contact him. After a while he stopped calling."

"I bet he found that strange."

"Probably."

"You may have hurt his feelings."

"I guess so."

"Why did you break it off so suddenly?"

"Because there was no need to keep acting."

"You mean there was no need to stay friends once you didn't have to act?"

"Yes, there was that," Kafuku said. "But there was another reason too."

"What was it?"

Kafuku fell silent. Misaki glanced at him occasionally, the unlit cigarette clamped between her lips.

"Go ahead and smoke if you want," Kafuku said.

"Huh?"

"You can light that thing."

"But the top is closed."

"I don't care."

Misaki lowered her window, lit the Marlboro with the car lighter, and took a deep drag. Her eyes narrowed in pleasure. She exhaled slowly, directing the smoke out the window.

"Tobacco's a killer," Kafuku said.

"Being alive is a killer, if you think about it," Misaki said.

Kafuku laughed. "That's one way to see it."

"That's the first time I've seen you laugh," Misaki said.

She had a point, Kafuku thought. It had been a long time indeed since he had laughed, not as an act, but for real.

"I've been meaning to tell you this for a while," he said. "But there's something very attractive about you. You're not homely at all, you know."

"Thank you very much. My features are plain, that's all. Like Sonya's."

Kafuku looked at Misaki in surprise. "I see you've read *Uncle Vanya*."

"I hear little bits of it every day, so I wanted to know

what it was about. I get curious too, you know," Misaki said. " 'Oh, how miserable I am! I can't stand it. Why was I born so poorly favored? The agony!' A sad play, isn't it."

"A sad play indeed," Kafuku said. " 'Oh, how unbearable! Is there no help for me? I am forty-seven now. If I live till sixty I have thirteen more years to endure. Too long. How shall I pass those thirteen years? What will help me get through the days?' People only lived to about sixty back then. Uncle Vanya was fortunate he wasn't born into today's world."

"You were born the same year as my father. I checked."

Kafuku didn't respond. He took a handful of cassettes and scanned the songs on the labels. But he didn't play one. Misaki was holding the lit cigarette in her left hand with her arm out the window. Only when the line of cars crept forward and she had to use both hands to steer and shift gears did she place it between her lips for a moment.

"To be honest, I wanted to punish that guy," Kafuku said, as if confessing to something. "The guy who slept with my wife." He put the cassettes back in their containers.

"Punish him?"

"Make him pay for what he did. My plan was to put him off his guard by pretending to be his friend, find his fatal flaw, and use it to torture him."

"What kind of fatal flaw?" Misaki asked, knitting her brow in thought.

"I didn't think that far ahead. He was a guy who let his defenses down when he drank, so I was sure something would turn up sooner or later. I could use whatever it was to cause a scandal—create a situation that would destroy his reputation. I figured it would be a piece of cake. Then when he went through his divorce arbitration, he'd probably lose the right to see his son, which would have been a terrible blow. I doubted he could recover from that."

"That's pretty dark."

"Yeah, it's dark for sure."

"And it was all to take revenge on him for sleeping with your wife?"

"It was slightly different from revenge," Kafuku said. "I wasn't able to forget what had taken place between them. I tried really hard. But I failed. The image of her in another man's arms was stuck in my mind, as real as life. As if there was a demon with nowhere else to go clinging to a corner of the ceiling, eyes fastened on me. After my wife's death, I expected the demon would disappear if I just waited long enough. But it didn't. Instead its presence grew even stronger. I had to get rid of it. To do that I had to let go of my rage."

Kafuku wondered why he was telling all this to a young woman from Junitakicho in Hokkaido, a girl young enough to be his daughter. Yet once he started, he found he couldn't stop.

"So you thought you'd try to punish him," the girl said.

"Yes, that's true."

"But you didn't, did you?"

"No, I didn't," Kafuku said.

Misaki looked relieved to hear that. She gave a small sigh and flicked her lit cigarette onto the road. He guessed that was what people did in Junitakicho.

"I can't explain it very well, but at a certain point a lot of things didn't seem like that big a deal anymore. Like the demon had left me all of a sudden," Kafuku said. "The rage vanished. Or maybe it was never rage in the first place."

"Whatever it was, I'm glad for your sake that it left. That you never seriously hurt anyone."

"I think so too."

"But you never did figure out why your wife slept with that guy, why it had to be him, did you?"

"No, I never grasped that. It's still a big question mark for me. He was a nice, uncomplicated guy. And I think he truly loved my wife. It wasn't just a romp in the hay for him. Her death hit him hard. So did being turned away from her sickbed at the end. But I couldn't help liking the guy, even thought we could become friends."

Kafuku broke off. He was trying to trace the evolution of his feelings to find the words that best matched.

"In fact, though, he was a man of little consequence. He had a good personality. He was handsome, with a winning smile. He got along with everybody. But he wasn't someone who commanded much respect. He was a weak man, and a second-rate actor. My wife, though, had a strong will and great depth of character. She was the type of person who could think things through on her own. So how could she fall for a nonentity like that and go to bed with him? It's still a thorn in my heart."

"It sounds like you feel insulted. Do you?"

Kafuku thought for a moment. She had a point. "You may be right," he said.

"Isn't it possible that your wife didn't fall for him at all?" Misaki said simply. "And that's why she slept with him?"

Kafuku looked at Misaki's profile as if gazing at a distant landscape. She worked the wipers a few times to remove the drops from the windshield. The newly installed blades squeaked like a pair of squabbling twins.

"Women can be like that," Misaki added.

Kafuku couldn't think of what to say. So he kept silent.

"To me, it's a kind of sickness. Thinking about it doesn't do much good. The way my father walked out on my mother and me, my mother's constant abuse—I blame the sickness for those things. There's no logic involved. All I can do is accept what they did and try to get on with my life."

"So then we're all actors," Kafuku said.

"Yes, I think that's true. To a point, anyway."

Kafuku settled back in the leather seat, closed his eyes, and tried to focus his mind on the sound of the engine when Misaki shifted gears. But he couldn't catch the precise moment. It was all too smooth, too mysterious. He could only make out a slight gradation in the engine's hum. It was like the wings of a flying insect, now drawing closer, now fading away.

Time to take a nap, Kafuku thought. Sleep deeply and wake up. Ten or fifteen minutes would be enough. Then back to the stage, and the acting. The bright lights, the rehearsed lines. The applause, the falling curtain. Leaving who one was for a brief time, then returning. But the self that one returned to was never exactly the same as the self that one had left behind.

"I'm going to sleep a little," Kafuku said.

Misaki didn't answer. She quietly studied the road. Kafuku was grateful for her silence.

Translated by Ted Goossen

YESTERDAY

AS FAR AS I KNOW, the only person ever to put Japanese lyrics to the Beatles song "Yesterday" (and to do so in the distinctive Kansai dialect, no less) was a guy named Kitaru. He used to belt out his own version when he was taking a bath.

> Yesterday
> Is two days before tomorrow,
> The day after two days ago.

This is how it began, as I recall, but I haven't heard it for a long time and I'm not positive that's how it went. From start to finish, though, Kitaru's lyrics were almost meaningless nonsense that had nothing to do with the original words. That familiar lovely, melancholy melody paired with the breezy Kansai dialect—which you might call the opposite of pathos—made for a strange combination, a bold denial of anything constructive. At least, that's how it sounded to me. At the time, I just listened and shook my head. I was able to laugh it off, but I also read a kind of hidden import in it.

To my ear, Kitaru had an almost pitch-perfect Kansai accent, even though he was born and raised in Denen-chofu, in Ota-ku, in Tokyo. As for me, although I was born and raised in Kansai, I spoke almost perfect standard (that is, Tokyo-style) Japanese. The two of us definitely made an odd pair.

I first met Kitaru at a coffee shop near the main gate of Waseda University, where we worked part time, I in the kitchen and Kitaru as a waiter. We used to talk a lot during downtime at the shop. We were both twenty, our birthdays only a week apart.

"Kitaru is an unusual last name," I said one day.

"Yeah, for sure," Kitaru replied in his heavy Kansai accent.

"The Lotte baseball team had a pitcher with the same name."

"The two of us aren't related. Not so common a name, though, so who knows? Maybe there's a connection somewhere."

I was a sophomore at Waseda then, in the literature department. Kitaru had failed the entrance exam and was attending a prep course to cram for the retake. He'd failed the exam twice, actually, but you wouldn't have guessed it by the way he acted. He didn't seem to put much effort into studying. When he was free, he read a lot, but nothing related to the exam—a biography of Jimi Hendrix, books of shogi problems, *Where Did the Universe Come From?* and the like. He told me that he commuted to the cram school from his parents' place in Ota Ward, in Tokyo.

"Ota Ward?" I asked, astonished. "But I was sure you were from Kansai."

"No way. Denenchofu, born and bred."

This really threw me.

"Then how come you speak Kansai dialect?" I asked.

"I acquired it. Just made up my mind to learn it."

"*Acquired* it?"

"Yeah, I studied hard, Verbs, nouns, accent—the whole nine yards. Same as studying English or French. Went to Kansai for training, even."

I was impressed. So there were people who studied the Kansai dialect as if it were a foreign language? That was news to me. It made me realize all over again how huge Tokyo was, and how many things there were that I didn't know. It reminded me of the novel *Sanshiro*, a typical country-boy-bumbles-his-way-around-the-big-city story.

"As a kid, I was a huge Hanshin Tigers fan," Kitaru explained. "Went to their games whenever they played in Tokyo. But if I sat in the Hanshin bleachers wearing their jerseys and spoke with a Tokyo dialect, nobody wanted to have anything to do with me. Couldn't be part of the community, y'know? So I figured, I gotta learn the Kansai dialect, and I worked like a dog to do just that."

"That was your motivation?" I could hardly believe it.

"Right. That's how much the Tigers mean to me," Kitaru said. "Now the Kansai dialect's all I speak—at school, at home, even when I talk in my sleep. My dialect's near perfect, don't you think?"

"Absolutely. I was positive you were from Kansai," I said. "But your version isn't the dialect from Hanshinkan—the Kobe area. It sounds more like it comes from hard-core, downtown Osaka."

"You picked up on that, huh? During summer break

in high school, I did a homestay in Tenojiku in Osaka. Great place. Can walk to the zoo and everything."

"Homestay?" Now that was impressive.

"If I'd put as much effort into studying for the entrance exams as I did into studying the Kansai dialect, I wouldn't be a two-time loser like I am now."

He had a point. Even his self-directed put-down was kind of Kansai-like.

"So where're you from?" he asked.

"Kansai. Near Kobe," I said.

"Near Kobe? Where?"

"Ashiya," I replied.

"Wow, nice place. Why didn't you say so from the start?"

I explained. When people asked me where I was from and I said Ashiya, they always assumed that my family was wealthy. But there were all types in Ashiya. My family, for one, wasn't particularly well off. My dad worked for a pharmaceutical company and my mom was a librarian. Our house was small and our car a cream-colored Corolla. So when people asked me where I was from I always said "near Kobe," so they didn't get any preconceived ideas about me.

"Man, sounds like you and me are the same," Kitaru said. "My address is Denenchofu—a pretty high-class place—but my house is in the shabbiest part of town. Shabby house as well. You should come over sometime. You'll be, like, 'Wha'? This is Denenchofu? No way!' But worrying about something like that makes no sense, yeah? It's just an address. I do the opposite—hit 'em right up front with the fact that I'm from *Den-en-cho-fu*. Like, how d'you like *that*, huh?"

I was impressed. And after this we became friends.

There were a couple of reasons why, when I came to Tokyo, I totally gave up speaking the Kansai dialect. Until I graduated from high school, I spoke nothing but—in fact, I'd never spoken standard Tokyo even once. But all it took was a month in Tokyo for me to become completely fluent in this new version of Japanese. I was kind of surprised that I could adapt so quickly. Maybe I'm a chameleon and I didn't even realize it. Or maybe my sense of language is more advanced than most people's. Either way, no one believed now that I was actually from Kansai.

Another reason I stopped using the Kansai dialect was that I wanted to become a totally different person.

When I moved from Kansai to Tokyo to start college, I spent the whole bullet-train ride mentally reviewing my eighteen years and realized that almost everything that had happened to me was pretty embarrassing. I'm not exaggerating. I didn't want to remember any of it—it was so pathetic. The more I thought about my life up to then, the more I hated myself. It wasn't that I didn't have a few good memories—I did. A handful of happy experiences. But if you added them up, the shameful, painful memories far outnumbered the others. When I thought of how I'd been living, how I'd been approaching life, it was all so trite, so miserably pointless. Unimaginative middle-class rubbish, and I wanted to gather it all up and stuff it away in some drawer. Or else light it on fire and watch it go up in smoke (though what kind of smoke it would emit I had no idea). Anyway, I wanted to get rid of it all and start a new life in Tokyo with a clean slate as a brand-new person. Try out the new possibilities of a new me. Jettisoning the Kansai dialect was a practical (as well as symbolic) method of accomplishing this. Because, in the final analysis, the language we speak constitutes who we are as people. At least that's the way it seemed to me at eighteen.

"Embarrassing? What was so embarrassing?" Kitaru asked me.

"You name it."

"Didn't get along with your folks?"

"We get along okay," I said. "But it was still embarrassing. Just being with them made me feel embarrassed."

"You're weird, y'know that?" Kitaru said. "What's so embarrassing about being with your folks? I have a good time with mine."

I couldn't really explain it. What's so bad about having a cream-colored Corolla? I couldn't say. The road in front of our place was kind of narrow, and my parents just weren't interested in spending money for the sake of appearances, that's all.

"My parents are on my case all the time 'cause I don't study enough. I hate it, but whaddaya gonna do? That's their job. You gotta look past that, y'know?"

"You're pretty easygoing, aren't you?" I said.

"You got a girl?" Kitaru asked.

"Not right now."

"But you had one before?"

"Until a little while ago."

"You guys broke up?"

"That's right," I said.

"Why'd you break up?"

"It's a long story. I don't want to get into it."

"A girl from Ashiya?" Kitaru asked.

"No, not from Ashiya. She lived in Shukugawa. It's nearby."

"She let you go all the way?"

I shook my head. "No, not all the way."

"That's why you broke up?"

I thought about it. "That's part of it."

"But she let you get to third base?"

"Rounding third base."

"How far'd you go, exactly?"

"I don't want to talk about it," I said.

"Is that one of those 'embarrassing things' you mentioned?"

"Yeah," I said. That was another thing I didn't want to remember.

"Man, complicated life you got there," Kitaru said.

The first time I heard Kitaru sing "Yesterday" with those crazy lyrics he was in the bath at his house in Denenchofu (which, despite his description, was not a shabby house in a shabby neighborhood but an ordinary house in an ordinary neighborhood, an older house, but bigger than my house in Ashiya, not a standout in any way—and, incidentally, the car in the driveway was a navy-blue Golf, a recent model). Whenever Kitaru came home, he immediately dropped everything and jumped in the bath. And, once he was in the tub, he stayed there forever. So I would often lug a little round stool to the adjacent changing room and sit there, talking to him through the sliding door that was open an inch or so. That was the only way to avoid listening to his mother drone on and on—mostly complaints about her weird son and how he needed to study more. That's where he sang the song with those absurd lyrics for me (though whether it was for my sake or not, I'm not sure).

"Those lyrics don't make any sense," I told him. "It just sounds like you're making fun of the song 'Yesterday.'"

"Don't be a smartass. I'm not making fun of it. Even if I was, you gotta remember that John loved nonsense and word games. Right?"

"But Paul's the one who wrote the words and music for 'Yesterday.'"

"You sure about that?"

"Absolutely," I declared. "Paul wrote the song and recorded it by himself in the studio with a guitar. A string quartet was added later, but the other Beatles weren't involved at all. They thought it was too wimpy for a Beatles song."

"Really? I'm not up on that kind of privileged information."

"It's not privileged information. It's a well-known fact," I said.

"Who cares? Those are just details," Kitaru's voice said calmly from a cloud of steam. "I'm singing in the bath in my own house. Not putting out a record or anything. I'm not violating any copyright, or bothering a soul. You've got no right to complain."

And he launched into the chorus, his voice carrying loud and clear, like people do when they're in the tub. He hit the high notes especially well. "Tho' she was here / Til yesterday . . ." Or something along those lines.

He lightly splashed the bathwater as an accompaniment. I probably should have interrupted him, sung along to encourage, but I just couldn't bring myself to. Sitting there, talking through a glass door to keep him company while he soaked in the tub for an hour, wasn't all that much fun.

"But how can you spend so long soaking in the bath?" I asked. "Doesn't your body get all swollen?"

I've never been able to spend much time in the bath. I get bored trying to sit still and soak. You can't read a book or listen to music, so I soon find myself at loose ends.

"When I soak in a bath for a long time, all kinds of good ideas suddenly come to me," Kitaru said.

"You mean like those lyrics to 'Yesterday'?"

"Well, that'd be one of them," Kitaru said.

"Instead of spending so much time thinking up ideas in the bath, shouldn't you be studying for the entrance exam?" I asked.

"Jeez, what a downer you are. My mom says exactly the same thing. Aren't you a little young to be, like, the voice of reason or something?"

"But you've been cramming for two years. Aren't you getting tired of it?"

"For sure. Of course I wanna be in college as soon as I can and have fun. And go out on some real dates with my girlfriend."

"Then why not study harder?"

"Yeah—well," he said, drawing the words out. "If I could do that, I'd be doing it already."

"College is a drag," I said. "I was totally disappointed once I got in. But not getting in would be even more of a drag."

"Fair enough," Kitaru said. "I got no comeback for that."

"So why don't you study?"

"Lack of motivation," he said.

"Motivation?" I said. "Shouldn't being able to go out on dates with your girlfriend be all the motivation you need?"

"I guess," Kitaru said. "Look, this could get pretty long if I get into it all. Thing is, it's like I'm divided into two parts inside me, you know?"

There was a girl Kitaru had known since they were in elementary school together. A childhood girlfriend, you could say. They'd been in the same grade in school, but unlike him she had gotten into Sophia University straight out of high school. She was now majoring in French literature and had joined the tennis club. He'd shown me a photograph of her, and she was stunning. A beautiful figure and a lively expression. But the two of them weren't seeing each other much these days. They'd talked it over and decided that it was better not to date until Kitaru had passed the entrance exams, so that he could focus on his studies. Kitaru had been the one who suggested this. "Okay," she'd said, "if that's what you want." They talked on the phone a lot but met at most once a week, and those meetings were more like interviews than regular dates. They'd have tea and catch up on what they'd each been doing. They'd hold hands and exchange a brief kiss, but that was as far as it went. Pretty old school.

Kitaru wasn't what you'd call handsome, but he was pleasant looking enough. He wasn't tall but he was slim, and his hair and clothes were simple and stylish. As long as he didn't say anything, you'd assume he was a sensitive, well-brought-up city boy. He and his girlfriend made a great-looking couple. His only possible defect was that his face, a bit too slender and delicate, could give the impression that he was lacking in personality or was wishy-washy. But the moment he opened his mouth, this overall positive effect collapsed like a sand castle under an exuberant Labrador retriever. People were dismayed by his Kansai dialect, which he delivered fluently, as if that weren't enough, in a slightly piercing, high-pitched voice. The mismatch with his looks was overwhelming. Even for me it was, at first, a little too much to handle.

"Hey, Tanimura, aren't you lonely without a girlfriend?" Kitaru asked me the next day.

"I don't deny it," I told him.

"Then how about you go out with *my* girl?"

I couldn't understand what he meant. "What do you mean—*go out* with her?"

"She's a great girl. Pretty, honest, smart like all get-out. You go out with her, you won't regret it. I guarantee it."

"I'm sure I wouldn't," I said. "But why would I go out with your girlfriend? It doesn't make sense."

" 'Cause you're a good guy," Kitaru said. "Otherwise I wouldn't suggest it."

That didn't explain anything. What kind of relationship could there possibly be between me being a good guy (assuming this was the case) and me going out with his girlfriend?

"Erika and I have spent almost our whole lives together so far. We've been in school together from the start. We sort of naturally became a couple, and everybody around us approved. Our friends, our parents, our teachers. A tight little couple, always together."

Kitaru clasped his hands to illustrate.

"If we'd both gone straight into college, our lives

would've been all warm and fuzzy, but I blew the entrance exam big time, and here we are. I'm not sure why, exactly, but things kept on getting worse. I'm not blaming anyone for that—it's all my fault."

I listened to him in silence.

"So I kinda split myself in two," Kitaru said. He pulled his hands apart.

Split himself in two? "How so?" I asked.

He stared at his palms for a moment, and then spoke. "What I mean is part of me's, like, worried, y'know? I mean, I'm going to some fricking cram school, studying for the fricking entrance exams, while Erika's having a ball in college. Playing tennis, doing whatever. She's got new friends, is probably dating some new guy, for all I know. When I think of all that, I feel left behind. Like my mind's in a fog. You know what I mean?"

"I guess so," I said.

"But another part of me is, like—relieved? If we'd just kept going like we were, with no problems or anything, a nice couple smoothly sailing through life, it's like—what's gonna happen to us? We have that kind of choice, I was thinking. You follow?"

"I do and I don't," I said.

"It's like, we graduate from college, get married, we're this wonderful married couple everybody's happy about, we have the typical two kids, put 'em in the good old Denenchofu elementary school, go out to the Tama River banks on Sundays, 'Ob-la-di, ob-la-da' . . . I'm not saying that kinda life's bad. But I wonder, y'know, if life should really be that easy, that comfortable. It might be better to go our separate ways for a while, and if we find out that we really can't get along without each other, then we get back together."

"So you're saying that things being smooth and comfortable is a problem. Is that it?"

"Yep, that's about the size of it."

I wasn't exactly following what was wrong with things being smooth and comfortable, but pursuing that looked tricky, so I gave it up. "But why do I have to go out with your girlfriend?" I asked.

"I figure, if she's gonna go out with other guys, it's better if it's you. 'Cause I know you. And you can gimme, like, updates and stuff."

That didn't make any sense to me, though I admit I was interested in the idea of meeting Erika. I also wanted to find out why a beautiful girl like her would want to go out with a weird character like Kitaru. I've always been a little shy around new people, but I never lack curiosity.

"How far have you gone with her?" I asked.

"You mean sex?" Kitaru said.

"Yeah. Have you gone all the way?"

Kitaru shook his head. "I just couldn't. I've known her since she was a kid, and it's kind of embarrassing, y'know, to act like we're just starting out, and take her clothes off, fondle her, touch her, whatever. If it were some other girl, I don't think I'd have a problem, but putting my hand in her underpants, even just thinking about doing it with her—I dunno—it just seems *wrong*. You know?"

I didn't.

"I kiss her, of course, and hold her hand. I've touched her breasts, through her clothes. But it's like we're just fooling around, y'know, playing. Even when we get a little worked up, there's never any sign like things'll go any further."

"Instead of waiting for signs or anything, shouldn't

you be the one to make things happen, and take the next step?" That's what people call sexual desire.

"Naw, it's like in our case things just don't go that way. I can't explain it well," Kitaru said. "Like, when you're jerking off, you picture some actual girl, yeah?"

"I suppose," I said.

"But I can't picture Erika. It's like doing that's wrong, y'know? So when I do it I think about some other girl. Somebody I don't really like that much. What do you think?"

I thought it over but couldn't reach any conclusion. Other people's masturbation habits were beyond me. There were things about my own that I couldn't fathom.

"Anyway, let's all get together once, the three of us," Kitaru said. "Then you can think it over."

The three of us—me, Kitaru, and his girlfriend, whose full name was Erika Kuritani—met on a Sunday afternoon in a coffee shop near Denenchofu Station. She was almost as tall as Kitaru, nicely tanned, and decked out in a neatly ironed short-sleeved white blouse and a navy-blue miniskirt. Like the perfect model of a respectable uptown college girl. She was as attractive as in her photograph, but when I saw her in the flesh what really drew me was less her looks than the kind of effortless vitality that seemed to radiate from her. She was the opposite of Kitaru, who paled a bit in comparison.

Kitaru introduced us. "I'm really happy that Aki-kun has a friend," Erika Kuritani told me. Kitaru's first name was Akiyoshi. She was the only person in the world who called him Aki-kun.

"Don't exaggerate. I got tons of friends," Kitaru said.

"No, you don't," Erika said. "A person like you can't make friends. You were born in Tokyo, yet all you speak is the Kansai dialect, and every time you open your mouth it's one annoying thing after another about the Hanshin Tigers or shogi moves. There's no way a weird person like you can get along well with normal people."

"Well, if you're gonna get into that, this guy's pretty weird, too." Kitaru pointed at me. "He's from Ashiya but only speaks the Tokyo dialect."

"That's much more common," Erika said. "At least more common than the opposite."

"Hold on, now—that's cultural discrimination," Kitaru said. "Cultures are all equal, y'know. The Tokyo dialect's no better than Kansai."

"Maybe they are equal," Erika insisted, "but since the Meiji Restoration the way people speak in Tokyo has been the standard for spoken Japanese. I mean, has anyone ever translated *Franny and Zooey* into the Kansai dialect?"

"If they did, I'd buy it, for sure," Kitaru said.

I probably would, too, I thought, but kept quiet. Best to mind my own business.

"Anyway, that's common knowledge now," she said. "You're narrow-minded, Aki-kun, and biased."

"What are you talking about, narrow-minded and biased? To me, cultural discrimination is a much more dangerous kind of bias."

Wisely, instead of being dragged deeper into that discussion, Erika Kuritani changed the subject.

"There's a girl in my tennis club who's from Ashiya, too," she said, turning to me. "Eiko Sakurai. Do you happen to know her?"

"I do," I said. Eiko Sakurai was a tall, gangly girl

whose parents operated a large golf course. Stuck-up, flat-chested, with a funny-looking nose and a none-too-wonderful personality. Tennis was the one thing she'd always been good at. If I never saw her again, it would be too soon for me.

"He's a nice guy, and he hasn't got a girlfriend right now," Kitaru said to Erika. He meant me. "His looks are okay, he has good manners, and he knows all kinds of things, reads these difficult books. He's neat and clean, as you can see, and doesn't have any terrible diseases. A promising young man, I'd say."

"All right," Erika said. "There are some really cute new members of our club I'd be happy to introduce him to."

"Nah, that's not what I mean," Kitaru said. "Could *you* go out with him? I'm not in college yet and I can't go out with you the way I'd like to. Instead of me, you could go out with *him*. And then I wouldn't have to worry."

"What do you mean, you wouldn't have to worry?" Erika asked.

"I mean, like, I know both of you, and I'd feel better if you went out with him instead of some guy I've never laid eyes on."

Erika stared at Kitaru as if she couldn't quite believe what she was seeing. Finally, she spoke. "So you're saying it's okay for me to go out with another guy if it's Tanimura-kun here? Because he's a *really nice guy*, you're seriously suggesting we go out, on a date?"

"Hey, it's not such a terrible idea, is it? Or are you already going out with some other guy?"

"No, there's no one else," Erika said in a quiet voice.

"Then why not go out with *him*? It can be a kinda cultural exchange."

"Cultural exchange," Erika repeated. She looked at me.

It didn't seem as though anything I said would help, so I kept silent. I held my coffee spoon in my hand, studying the design on it, like a museum curator scrutinizing an artifact from an Egyptian tomb.

"*Cultural exchange?* What's that supposed to mean?" she asked Kitaru.

"Like, bringing in another viewpoint might not be so bad for us—"

"That's your idea of cultural exchange?"

"Yeah, what I mean is—"

"All right," Erika Kuritani said firmly. If there had been a pencil nearby, I might have picked it up and snapped it in two. "If you think we should do it, Aki-kun, then okay. A cultural exchange it is."

She took a sip of tea, returned the cup to the saucer, turned to me, and smiled. "Since Aki-kun has recommended we do this, Tanimura-kun, let's go on a date. Sounds like fun. When are you free?"

I couldn't speak. Not being able to find the right words at crucial times is one of my many problems. A basic problem that changing locations and languages doesn't solve.

Erika took a red leather planner from her bag, opened it, and checked her schedule. "How is this Saturday?" she asked.

"I have no plans," I said.

"Saturday it is, then. Where shall we go?"

"He likes movies," Kitaru told her. "His dream is to write screenplays someday. He's in a screenwriting workshop."

"Then let's go see a movie. What kind of movie should we see? I'll let you decide that, Tanimura-kun. I don't like horror films, but other than that anything's fine."

"She's really a scaredy-cat," Kitaru said to me. "When we were kids and went to the haunted house at Korakuen, she had to hold my hand and—"

"After the movie let's have a nice meal together," Erika said, cutting him off. She wrote her phone number down on a sheet from her notebook and passed it to me. "When you decide the time and place, could you give me a call?"

I didn't have a phone back then (this was long before cell phones were even a glimmer on the horizon), so I gave her the number for the coffee shop where Kitaru and I worked. I glanced at my watch.

"I'm sorry but I've got to get going," I said, as cheerfully as I could manage. "I have this report I have to finish up by tomorrow."

"Can't it wait?" Kitaru said. "We only just got here. Why don't you stay so we can talk some more? There's a great noodle shop right around the corner."

Erika didn't express an opinion. I put the money for my coffee on the table and stood up. "It's an important report," I explained, "so I really can't put it off." Actually, it didn't matter all that much.

"I'll call you tomorrow or the day after," I told Erika.

"I'll be looking forward to it," she said, a wonderful smile rising to her lips. A smile that, to me at least, seemed a little too good to be true.

I left the coffee shop, and as I walked to the station I wondered what the hell I was doing. Brooding over how things had turned out—after everything had already been decided—was another of my chronic problems.

.   .   .

That Saturday, Erika and I met in Shibuya and saw a Woody Allen film set in New York. Somehow I'd gotten the sense that she might be fond of Woody Allen movies. And I was pretty sure that Kitaru had never taken her to see one. Luckily, it was a good movie, and we were both in a good mood when we left the theater.

We strolled around the twilight streets for a while, then went to a small Italian place in Sakuragaoka and had pizza and Chianti. It was a casual, moderately priced restaurant. Subdued lighting, candles on the tables. (Most Italian restaurants at the time had candles on the tables and checked gingham tablecloths.) We talked about all kinds of things, the sort of conversation you'd expect two college sophomores on a first date to have (assuming you could actually call this a date). The movie we'd just seen, our college life, hobbies. We enjoyed talking more than I'd expected, and she even laughed out loud a couple of times. I don't want to sound like I'm bragging, but I seem to have a knack for getting girls to laugh.

"I heard from Aki-kun that you broke up with your high school girlfriend not long ago?" Erika asked me.

"Yeah," I replied. "We went out for almost three years, but it didn't work out. Unfortunately."

"Aki-kun said things didn't work out with her because of sex. That she didn't—how should I put it?—give you what you wanted?"

"That was part of it. But not all. If I'd really loved her, I think I could have been patient. If I'd been sure that I loved her, I mean. But I wasn't."

Erika Kuritani nodded.

"Even if we'd gone all the way, things most likely would have ended up the same," I said. "That became increasingly obvious after I moved to Tokyo and put some distance between us. I'm sorry things didn't work out, but I think it was inevitable."

"Is it hard on you?" she asked.

"Is *what* hard?"

"Suddenly being on your own after being a couple."

"Sometimes," I said honestly.

"But maybe going through that kind of tough, lonely experience is necessary when you're young? Part of the process of growing up?"

"You think so?"

"The way surviving hard winters makes a tree grow stronger, the growth rings inside it tighter."

I tried to imagine growth rings inside me. But the only thing I could picture was a leftover slice of Baum-kuchen cake, the kind with treelike rings inside.

"I agree that people need that sort of period in their lives," I said. "It's even better if they know that it'll end someday."

She smiled. "Don't worry. I know you'll meet somebody nice soon."

"I hope so," I said.

Erika Kuritani mulled over something for a while. I helped myself to the pizza in the meantime.

"Tanimura-kun, I wanted to ask your advice on something. Is it okay?"

"Sure," I said. Uh-oh, I thought, what have I gotten myself into? This was another problem I often had to deal with: people I'd just met wanting my advice about something important. And I was pretty sure that what Erika Kuritani wanted my advice about wasn't very pleasant.

"I'm confused," she began.

Her eyes shifted back and forth, like those of a cat in search of something.

"I'm sure you know this already, but though Aki-kun's in his second year of cramming for the entrance exams, he barely studies. He skips exam-prep school a lot, too. So I'm sure he'll fail again next year. If he aimed for a lower-tier school, he could get in somewhere, but he has his heart set on Waseda. He's convinced it's Waseda or nothing. I think that's a pointless way of thinking, but he doesn't listen to me, or to his parents. It's become like an obsession for him . . . But if he really feels that way he should study hard so that he can pass the Waseda exam, and he doesn't."

"Why doesn't he study more?"

"He truly believes that he'll pass the entrance exam if luck is on his side," Erika said. "That studying is a waste of time, a waste of his life. I find that way of thinking unbelievable."

That's one way of looking at it, I thought, but didn't share my analysis with her.

Erika Kuritani sighed and went on, "In elementary school he was really good at studying. Always at the top of his class academically. But once he got to junior high his grades started to slide. He was a bit of a child prodigy—his personality just isn't suited to the daily grind of studying. He'd rather go off and do crazy things on his own. I'm the exact opposite. I'm not all that bright, but I always buckle down and get the job done."

I hadn't studied very hard myself and had gotten into college on the first try. Maybe luck had been on my side.

"I'm very fond of Aki-kun," she continued. "He's got a lot of wonderful qualities. But sometimes it's hard for me to go along with his extreme way of thinking. Take this thing with the Kansai dialect. Why does somebody who was born and raised in Tokyo go to the trouble of learning the Kansai dialect and speak it all the time? I don't get it, I really don't. At first I thought it was a joke, but it isn't. He's dead serious."

"I think he wants to have a different personality, to be somebody different from who he's been up till now," I said.

"That's why he only speaks the Kansai dialect?"

"I agree with you that it's a radical way of dealing with it."

Erika picked up a slice of pizza and bit off a piece the size of a large postage stamp. She chewed it thoughtfully before she spoke.

"Tanimura-kun, I'm asking this because I don't have anyone else to ask. You don't mind?"

"Of course not," I said. What else could I say?

"As a general rule," she said, "when a guy and a girl go out for a long time and get to know each other really well, the guy has a physical interest in the girl, right?"

"As a general rule, I'd say so, yes."

"If they kiss, he'll want to go further?"

"Normally, sure."

"You feel that way, too?"

"Of course," I said.

"But Aki-kun doesn't. When we're alone, he doesn't want to go any further."

It took a while for me to choose the right words. "That's a personal thing," I said finally. "People have different ways of getting what they want. It really depends on the person. Kitaru likes you a lot—that's a given—but your relationship is so close and comfortable he may not be able to take things to the next level, the way most people do."

"You really think so?"

I shook my head. "To tell the truth, I don't really understand it. I've never experienced it myself. I'm just saying that could be one possibility."

"Sometimes it feels like he doesn't have any sexual desire for me."

"I'm sure he does. But it might be a little embarrassing for him to admit it."

"But we're twenty, adults already. Old enough not to be embarrassed."

"The rate at which time progresses might be a little 'off,' depending on the person," I said.

Erika thought about this. She seemed to be the type who always tackles things head on.

"I think Kitaru is honestly seeking something," I went on. "In his own way, at his own pace, very genuinely and directly. It's just that I don't think he's grasped yet what it is. That's why he can't make any progress, and that applies to all kinds of things. If you don't know what you're looking for, it's not easy to look for it."

Erika raised her head and stared me right in the eye. The candle flame was reflected in her dark eyes, a small, brilliant point of light. It was so beautiful I had to look away.

"Of course, you know him much better than I do," I averred.

She sighed again.

"Actually, I'm seeing another guy besides Aki-kun," she said. "A boy in my tennis club who's a year ahead of me."

It was my turn to remain silent.

"I truly love Aki-kun, and I don't think I could ever feel the same way about anybody else. Whenever I'm away from him I get this terrible ache in my chest, always in the same spot. It's true. There's a place in my heart reserved just for him. But at the same time I have this strong *urge* inside me to try something else, to come into contact with all kinds of people. Call it curiosity, a thirst to know more. More possibilities. It's a natural emotion and I can't suppress it, no matter how much I try."

I pictured a healthy plant outgrowing the pot it had been planted in.

"When I say I'm confused, that's what I mean," Erika Kuritani said.

"Then you should tell Kitaru exactly how you feel," I said. "If you hide it from him that you're seeing someone else, and he happens to find out anyway, it'll hurt him. You don't want that."

"But can he accept that? The fact that I'm going out with someone else?"

"I imagine he'll understand how you feel," I said.

"You think so?"

"I do," I said.

I figured that Kitaru would understand her confusion, because he was feeling the same thing. In that sense, they really were on the same wavelength. Still, I wasn't entirely confident that he would calmly accept what she was actually doing (or *might* be doing). He didn't seem that strong a person to me. But it would be even harder for him if she kept a secret from him or lied to him.

Erika Kuritani stared silently at the candle flame flickering in the breeze from the AC. "I often have the same dream," she said. "Aki-kun and I are on a ship. A long journey on a large ship. We're together in a small cabin, it's late at night, and through the porthole we can see the full moon. But that moon is made of pure, transparent ice. And the bottom half of it is sunk in the sea. 'That looks like the moon,' Aki-kun tells me, 'but it's really made of ice and is only about eight inches thick. So when the sun comes out in the morning it all melts. Best to get a good look at it now, while you have the chance.' I've had this dream so many times. It's a beautiful dream. Always the same moon. Always eight inches thick. The bottom half is sunk down in the sea. I'm leaning against Aki-kun, the moon shines beautifully, it's just the two of us, the waves lapping gently outside. But every time I wake up I feel unbearably sad. That moon made of ice is nowhere to be found."

Erika Kuritani was silent for a time. Then she spoke again. "I think how wonderful it would be if Aki-kun and I could continue on that voyage forever. Every night we'd snuggle close and gaze out the porthole at that moon made of ice. Come morning the moon would melt away, and at night it would reappear. But maybe that's not the case. Maybe one night the moon wouldn't be there. It scares me to think that. I wonder what kind of dream I'll have the next day and I get so frightened it's like I can actually hear my body shrinking."

When I saw Kitaru at the coffee shop the next day, he asked me how the date had gone.

"You kiss her?"

"No way," I said.

"Don't worry—I'm not gonna freak if you did," he said.

"I didn't do anything like that."

"Didn't hold her hand?"

"No, I didn't hold her hand."

"So what'd you do?"

"We went to see a movie, took a walk, had dinner, and talked," I said.

"That's it?"

"Usually you don't try to move too fast on a first date."

"Really?" Kitaru said. "I've never been out on a regular date, so I don't know."

"But I enjoyed being with her. If she were my girlfriend, I'd never let her out of my sight."

Kitaru considered this. He was about to say something but thought better of it. "So what'd you eat?" he asked finally.

I told him about the pizza and the Chianti.

"Pizza and Chianti?" He sounded surprised. "I never knew she liked pizza. We've only been to, like, noodle shops and cheap diners. Wine? I didn't even know she could drink."

Kitaru never touched liquor himself.

"There are probably quite a few things you don't know about her," I said.

I answered all his questions about the date. About the Woody Allen film (at his insistence I reviewed the whole plot), the meal (how much the bill came to, whether we split it or not), what she had on (white cotton dress, hair pinned up), what kind of underwear she wore (how would I know that?), what we talked about. I said nothing about her going out with another guy. Nor did I mention her dreams of an icy moon.

"You guys decide when you'll have a second date?"

"No, we didn't," I said.

"Why not? You liked her, didn't you?"

"She's great. But we can't go on like this. I mean, she's *your* girlfriend, right? You say it's okay to kiss her, but there's no way I can do that."

More pondering by Kitaru. "Y'know something?" he said finally. "I've been seeing a therapist since the end of junior high. My parents and teachers, they all said to go to one. 'Cause I used to do things at school from time to time. You know—not *normal* kinds of things. But going to a therapist hasn't helped, far as I can see. It sounds good in theory, but therapists don't give a crap. They look at you like they know what's going on, then make you talk on and on and just listen. Man, *I* could do *that*."

"You're still seeing a therapist?"

"Yeah. Twice a month. Like throwing your money away, if you ask me. Erika didn't tell you about it?"

I shook my head.

"Tell you the truth, I don't know what's so weird about my way of thinking. To me, it seems like I'm just doing ordinary things in an ordinary way. But people tell me that almost everything I do is weird."

"Well, there are some things about you that are definitely not normal," I said.

"Like what?"

"Like your Kansai dialect. For someone from Tokyo who learned it by studying, it's just too perfect."

"You could be right," Kitaru admitted. "That is a little out of the ordinary."

"It might give people the creeps."

"Hmm. Could be."

"Normal people wouldn't take things that far."

"Yeah, you're probably right."

"But, as far as I can tell, even if what you do isn't normal, it's not bothering anybody."

"Not right now."

"So what's wrong with that?" I said. I might have been a little upset then (at what or whom I couldn't say). I could feel my tone getting rough around the edges. "Who says there's anything wrong with *that*? If you're not bothering anybody *right now*, then so what? Who knows anything beyond *right now* anyway? You want to speak the Kansai dialect, then you *should*. Go for it. You don't want to study for the entrance exam? Then don't. Don't feel like sticking your hand inside Erika Kuritani's panties? Who's saying you have to? It's your life. You should do what you want and forget about what other people think."

Kitaru, mouth slightly open, stared at me in amazement. "You know something, Tanimura? You're a good guy. Though sometimes a little *too* normal, you know?"

"What're you gonna do?" I said. "You can't just change your personality."

"Exactly. You can't change your personality. That's what I'm trying to say."

"But Erika Kuritani is a great girl," I said. "She really cares about you. Whatever you do, don't let her go. You'll never find such a great girl again."

"I know. You don't gotta tell me," Kitaru said. "But just knowing isn't gonna help."

"Hey, how about giving someone else a chance to point that out?"

·　　·　　·

About two weeks later, Kitaru quit working at the coffee shop. I say quit, but he just suddenly stopped showing up. He didn't get in touch, didn't mention anything about taking time off. And this was during our busiest season, so the owner was pretty pissed. Kitaru was being so "totally irresponsible," as he put it. He was owed a week's pay, but he didn't come to pick it up. The owner asked me if I knew his address, but I told him I didn't. I didn't know either his phone number or his address. All I knew was roughly where to find his house in Denenchofu, and Erika Kuritani's home phone number.

Kitaru didn't say a word to me about quitting his job, and didn't get in touch after that. He simply vanished. I have to say it hurt me. I'd thought we were good friends, and it was tough to be cut off so completely like that. I didn't have any other friends in Tokyo.

The one thing that did concern me was how, the last two days before he disappeared, Kitaru had been unusually quiet. He wouldn't say much when I talked to him. And then he went and vanished. I could have called Erika Kuritani to check on his whereabouts, but somehow I couldn't bring myself to. I figured that what went on between the two of them was their business, and that it wasn't a healthy thing for me to get any more involved than I was. Somehow I had to get by in the narrow little world I belonged to.

After all this happened, for some reason I kept thinking about my ex-girlfriend. Probably I'd felt something, seeing Kitaru and Erika together. I wrote her a long letter apologizing for how I'd behaved. I could have been a whole lot kinder to her. But I never got a reply.

. . .

I recognized Erika Kuritani right away. I'd only seen her twice, and sixteen years had passed since then. But there was no mistaking her. She was still lovely, with the same lively, animated expression. She was wearing a black lace dress, with black high heels and two strands of pearls around her slim neck. She remembered me right away, too. We were at a wine-tasting party at a hotel in Akasaka. It was a black-tie event, and I had put on a dark suit and tie for the occasion. She was a rep for the advertising firm that was sponsoring the event, and was clearly doing a great job of handling it. It'd take too long to get into the reasons why I was there.

"Tanimura-kun, how come you never got in touch with me after that night we went out?" she asked. "I was hoping we could talk some more."

"You were a little too beautiful for me," I said.

She smiled. "That's nice to hear, even if you're just flattering me."

"I've never flattered anyone in my whole life," I said.

Her smile deepened. But what I'd said was neither a lie nor flattery. She was too gorgeous for me to be seriously interested in her. Back then, and even now. Plus her smile was a little too amazing to be real.

"I called that coffee shop you used to work at, but they said you didn't work there anymore," she said.

After Kitaru left, the job became a total bore, and I quit two weeks later.

Erika and I briefly reviewed the lives we'd led over the past sixteen years. After college, I was hired by a small publisher, but quit after three years and had been a writer ever since. I got married at twenty-seven but didn't have any children yet. Erika was still single. "They drive me so hard at work," she joked, "that I have no time to get married." I surmised that she'd had a number of affairs over the years. There was something about her, some aura radiating from her, that made me sure. She was the first one to bring up the topic of Kitaru.

"Aki-kun is working as a sushi chef in Denver now," she said.

"Denver?"

"Denver, Colorado. At least, according to the post-card he sent me a couple of months ago."

"Why Denver?"

"I don't know," Erika said. "The postcard before that was from Seattle. He was a sushi chef there, too. That was about a year ago. He sends me postcards sporadi-cally. Always some silly card with just a couple of lines dashed off. Sometimes he doesn't even write his return address."

"A sushi chef," I mused. "So he never did go to college?"

She shook her head. "At the end of that summer, I think it was, he suddenly announced that he'd had it with studying for the entrance exams. It's just a waste of time to keep on doing this, he said. And he went off to a cooking school in Osaka. Said he really wanted to learn Kansai cuisine and go to games at Koshien Stadium, the Hanshin Tigers' stadium. Of course, I asked him, 'How can you decide something so important like that and never ask me? What about *me*?' "

"And what did he say to that?"

She didn't respond. She just held her lips tight. She seemed about to say something, but it looked like if she did, she would cry. She managed to hold back the tears, as if wanting to avoid, above all, ruining her delicate eye makeup. I quickly changed the subject.

"When we went to that Italian restaurant in Shibuya, I remember we had cheap Chianti. Now look at us, tasting premium Napa wines. Kind of a strange twist of fate."

"I remember," she said, pulling herself together. "We saw a Woody Allen movie. Which one was it again?"

I told her.

"That was a great movie."

I agreed. It was definitely one of Woody Allen's masterpieces.

"Did things work out with that guy in your tennis club you were seeing?" I asked.

She shook her head. "No. We just didn't connect the way I thought we would. We went out for six months and then broke up."

"Can I ask a question?" I said. "It's very personal, though."

"Of course. I hope I can answer it."

"I don't want you to be offended."

"I'll do my best."

"You slept with that guy, right?"

Erika looked at me in surprise, her cheeks reddening.

"Why are you bringing that up now?"

"Good question," I said. "It's just been on my mind for a long time. But that was a weird thing to ask. I'm sorry."

Erika shook her head slightly. "No, it's okay. I'm not offended. I just wasn't expecting it. It was all so long ago."

I looked around the room. People in formal wear were scattered about. Corks popped one after another from expensive bottles of wine. A female pianist was playing "Like Someone in Love."

"The answer is yes," Erika Kuritani said. "I had sex with him a number of times."

"Curiosity, a thirst to know more," I said.

She gave a hint of a smile. "That's right. Curiosity, a thirst to know more."

"That's how we develop our growth rings."

"If you say so," she said.

"And I'm guessing that the first time you slept with him was soon after we had our date in Shibuya?"

She turned a page in her mental record book. "I think so. About a week after that. I remember that whole time pretty well. It was the first time I had 'that kind' of experience."

"And Kitaru was pretty quick on the uptake," I said, gazing into her eyes.

She looked down and fingered the pearls on her necklace one by one, as if making sure that they were all still there. She gave a small sigh, perhaps remembering something. "Yes, you're right about that. Aki-kun had a very strong sense of intuition."

"But it didn't work out with the other man."

She nodded. "Unfortunately, I'm just not that smart. I needed to take the long way around. I always take a roundabout way."

That's what we all do: endlessly take the long way around. I wanted to tell her this, but kept silent. Blurting out aphorisms like that was another one of my problems.

"Is Kitaru married?"

"As far as I know, he's still single," Erika said. "At least, he hasn't told me that he got married. Maybe the two of us are the type who will never make a go of marriage."

"Or maybe you're just taking a roundabout way of getting there."

"Perhaps."

"Is it out of the realm of possibility that the two of you might meet up again and get together?"

She smiled, looked down, and shook her head. I couldn't tell what that gesture meant. Maybe that this was not a possibility. Or else that it was pointless to even think about it.

"Do you still dream about the moon made of ice?" I asked.

Her head snapped up and she stared at me. Very calmly, slowly, a smile spread across her face. A completely natural, open smile.

"You remember my dream?" she asked.

"For some reason, I do."

"Even though it's someone else's dream?"

"Dreams are the kind of things you can—when you need to—borrow and lend out," I said. I really do overplay these sayings sometimes.

"That's a wonderful idea," she said. The smile still graced her face.

Someone called her name from behind me. It was time for her to get back to work.

"I don't have that dream anymore," she said in parting. "But I still remember every detail. What I saw, the way I felt. I can't forget it. I probably never will."

Erika Kuritani looked past me, staring off in the distance for a moment, as if searching the night sky for a moon made of ice. She abruptly turned and walked away. Off to the ladies' room, I imagined, to touch up her mascara.

When I'm driving and the Beatles song "Yesterday" comes on the radio, I can't help but hear those crazy lyrics Kitaru crooned in the bath. And I regret not writing them down. The lyrics were so weird that I remembered them for a while, but gradually my memory started to fade until finally I had nearly forgotten them. All I recall now are fragments, and I'm not even sure if these are actually what Kitaru sang. As time passes, memory, inevitably, reconstitutes itself.

When I was twenty or so, I tried several times to keep a diary, but I just couldn't do it. So many things were happening around me back then that I could barely keep up with them, let alone stand still and write them all down in a notebook. And most of these things weren't the kind that made me think, Oh, I've got to write this down. It was all I could do to open my eyes in the strong headwind, catch my breath, and forge ahead.

But, oddly enough, I remember Kitaru so well. We were friends for just a few months, yet every time I hear "Yesterday" scenes and conversations with him well up in my mind. The two of us talking while he soaked in the bath at his home in Denenchofu. Talking about the Hanshin Tigers' batting order, how troublesome certain aspects of sex could be, how mind-numbingly boring it was to study for the entrance exams, the history of the Denenchofu public elementary school, the emotional richness of the Kansai dialect. And I remember the strange date with Erika Kuritani. And what Erika—over the candlelit table at the Italian restaurant—confessed. It feels as though these things happened just yesterday. Music has that power to revive memories, sometimes so intensely that they hurt.

But when I look back at myself at age twenty, what I remember most is being alone and lonely. I had no girl-friend to warm my body or my soul, no friends I could open up to. No clue what I should do every day, no vision for the future. For the most part, I remained hidden away, deep within myself. Sometimes I'd go a week without talking to anybody. That kind of life continued for a year. A long, long year. Whether this period was a cold winter that left valuable growth rings inside me, I can't really say.

At the time I felt as if every night I, too, were gazing out a porthole at a moon made of ice. A transparent, eight-inch-thick, frozen moon. But no one was beside me. I watched that moon alone, unable to share its cold beauty with anyone.

Yesterday
Is two days before tomorrow,
The day after two days ago.

I hope that in Denver (or some other faraway town) Kitaru is happy. If it's too much to ask that he's *happy*, I hope at least that today he has his health, and all his needs met. For no one knows what kind of dreams tomorrow will bring.

Translated by Philip Gabriel

AN INDEPENDENT ORGAN

THERE ARE PEOPLE in the world who—thanks to a lack of intellectual acuity—live a life that is surprisingly artificial. I haven't run across all that many, but there are certainly a few. And Dr. Tokai was one of them.

In order for these so-called principled souls to survive in this warped world, these sort of people need to carefully adjust every day, though in most cases they're not consciously aware of the tiresome level of finesse necessary to do so. They're thoroughly convinced that they're perfectly guileless people who live honest lives devoid of ulterior motives or artifice. And when, by some chance, a special light shines on them, revealing how artificial and *unreal* the inner workings of their lives really are, circumstances can take a tragic, or in some cases comic, turn. Of course, there are many such people—we can call them blessed—who never encounter that light, or who see it but come away unfazed.

I'd like to record everything that I learned about this man named Tokai. Most of it originates from things he told me directly, though certain parts are based on information that people close to him told me, people he trusted. Admittedly, a certain amount is also conjecture, based on my own observations of things I thought might be true. Like soft pâté nicely filling in the gaps between one fact and another. In other words, the portrait that follows is not based entirely on fact. As the writer of this account, I cannot recommend that the reader treat it like evidence submitted in a trial, or supporting documents for a business transaction (though what sort of business transaction this could possibly be, I haven't a clue).

But if you slowly take a few steps back (making certain beforehand, mind you, that you're not standing in front of a cliff) and view this portrait from a distance, I'm sure you'll understand that the veracity of each tiny detail really isn't critical. All that matters is that a clear portrait of Dr. Tokai should emerge. At least, that's my hope, as the writer. He was, in short—how best to put this?—not the sort of person with an excessive amount of *room for misunderstanding*.

Not to say that he was a simple, accessible individual. In certain ways he was a complex, layered person, hard to grasp. I have no way of knowing what darkness lay in his subconscious, or what sins he may have carried with him. Still, based on his consistent patterns of behavior, composing an accurate overall picture is relatively easy. As a professional writer this may be a little presumptuous of me, but that's the impression I got at the time.

Tokai is fifty-two, and has never been married, or even lived with a woman. He lives in a two-bedroom apartment on the sixth floor of an elegant building in the tony Azabu district in Tokyo. A confirmed bachelor, you might say. He takes cares of most household chores himself—cooking, laundry, ironing, cleaning—and the rest are handled by professional housecleaners who come twice a month. He's basically a tidy person, so it's not hard to keep his house clean. When necessary, he can whip up delicious cocktails, and manages to cook most dishes, from *nikujaga* stew to sea bass *en papillote*. (Like most people who enjoy cooking, he spares no expense, so the dishes he prepares use the best ingredients and are always delicious.) He never felt he needed a woman around the house, never felt bored spending time alone, and hardly ever felt lonely sleeping by himself. Up to a certain point, that is.

He's a cosmetic plastic surgeon and runs the Tokai Beauty Clinic in Roppongi, which he inherited from his father. Naturally he has lots of opportunities to meet women. He isn't what you would call handsome, but has decent features—he never once considered getting plastic surgery himself—and, as the clinic does very well, he receives a high salary. He is well brought up, with good manners and a keen interest in culture, never at a loss for conversational topics. He still has a full head of hair (though some gray is starting to show), and though he's starting to put on a few pounds, regular workouts at the gym help him maintain a youthful physique. People might react negatively to this candor, but he has never lacked for women to date.

For some reason, ever since he was young, Tokai never wanted to get married and have a family. He was quite positive he wasn't suited for married life. So no matter how appealing the woman, if she was on the lookout for a permanent mate he kept his distance. As a result, most of the women he chose as girlfriends were either already married or had another primary boyfriend. As long as he maintained this arrangement, none of his partners had the desire to marry him. To put a finer point on it, Tokai was always a casual number-two lover, a convenient rainy-day boyfriend, or else a handy partner for a casual fling. And truthfully, Tokai was in his element in this kind of relationship, which for him was the most comfortable way to be with women. Any other arrangement—the kind where the woman sought a real partner—made him uncomfortable and on edge.

It didn't particularly bother him that these women made love to men other than him. Physical relations were, after all, just physical. As a doctor, this is what Tokai believed, and the women he dated felt the same. Tokai just hoped that when he was with a woman, she thought only of him. What she did or thought outside of their time together was her own business, not something for him to speculate about. Meddling in their lives outside the confines of their affair was out of the question.

For Tokai, having dinner with these women, drinking wine with them, and talking together was a distinct pleasure. Sex was merely an added pleasure, but never the ultimate goal. What he sought most was an intimate, intellectual connection with a number of attractive women. What came after that just happened. Because of this, women found themselves naturally attracted to him, enjoyed spending time with him, and often took the initiative. Personally, I think most women in the world (particularly the really attractive ones) are fed up with men who are always panting to get them into bed.

Tokai sometimes thought he should have kept track

of how many women he'd had this sort of relationship with over the course of nearly thirty years. But he was never all that interested in quantity. Quality of experience was the goal. And he wasn't that particular about a woman's physical appearance. As long as there wasn't some major flaw that aroused his professional interest, and as long as her looks weren't so boring as to make him yawn, that was enough. If you were worried about your looks, and had enough money saved up, you could alter your appearance pretty much any way you liked (as a specialist in that field, he knew of numerous remarkable examples). What he valued instead were bright, quick-witted women with a sense of humor. If a woman was very beautiful but had nothing to say, or no opinions of her own, Tokai became discouraged. No operation could ever improve a woman's intellectual skills. Having a pleasant conversation over dinner with an intelligent woman, or lingering over small talk while holding one another in bed—these were the moments he treasured.

Never once did he have any serious troubles with women, which was a good thing, because sticky emotional conflicts were definitely not for him. If, for some reason, the ominous dark clouds of impending friction appeared on the horizon, he knew how to skillfully back out of the relationship, careful not to aggravate things, and also careful not to hurt the woman. He did this swiftly and naturally, like a shadow drawn up into the gathering twilight. As a veteran bachelor he was well acquainted with the essential techniques.

He broke off relations with his girlfriends on a pretty regular basis. Most of the women with other boyfriends would, at a certain point in the relationship, say, "I'm very sorry, but I can't see you anymore. I'm getting married soon." In most cases the decision to get married came just before they were about to turn thirty, or forty. Just like calendars that sell well at the end of the year. Tokai always took the news calmly, with a suitably rueful smile. It was a shame, but what could you do? Matrimony wasn't for him, yet it was, in its way, a sacred institution, one that had to be respected.

At those times he would buy the woman an expensive wedding present. "Congratulations on your marriage," he'd tell her. "You're such an intelligent, charming, lovely woman. I hope you are truly happy—you deserve to be." And he really felt this way. These women had shared a precious portion of their lives with him and, out of what he hoped was genuine affection, provided him with some warm and wonderful times. For that alone he was grateful. What more could he ask of them?

But nearly a third of these women who went off to tie the sacred matrimonial knot ended up, some years later, phoning Tokai and asking to see him again. And he was always happy enough to have a pleasant—and certainly not very sacred—relationship with them. They transitioned from a casual relationship between two singles to the more complex relationship between a single man and a married woman—which made it all the more enjoyable. What they actually did together was pretty much the same as before, albeit a bit more competently. The remaining two-thirds of the women who got married never got in touch, and he never saw them again. They were, he surmised, living happy, fulfilling married lives, as wonderful wives and, he imagined, with a couple of children. If that was the case, Tokai was happy for them.

At this very moment a baby might be nursing at the marvelous breasts he used to lovingly stroke.

Most of Tokai's friends were married, with children. He'd visited their homes any number of times, but never once envied them. When their children were little, he found them cute, but once they were in junior high or high school, every single one of them turned rude, hated adults, and caused all kinds of problems in their efforts to rebel against their parents, relentlessly trying their parents' nerves and stomachs. The parents could only think of their children's academic performances and how to get their kids into top schools, so their bad grades became a running battle between the parents. The kids hardly opened their mouths at home, instead choosing to hole up in their rooms to chat online with their friends or obsess over some less-than-wholesome online porn. Tokai couldn't bring himself to want children like that. His friends all insisted that, when all was said and done, having children was a wonderful thing, but he never could buy this sales pitch. They probably just wanted Tokai to shoulder the same burden they dragged around. They selfishly were convinced that everyone else in the world should be obliged to suffer the way they did.

I myself married young and have stayed married ever since, but I happen not to have any children. So to a certain extent I can understand his view, though I do see it as a bit simplistic, a rhetorical exaggeration. I sometimes think that he might actually be right. Though, of course, not all cases are so miserable. In this huge world there are some beautiful, happy families where parents and children maintain a close, warm relationship—a situation about as frequent as hat tricks in soccer. I have no confidence at all that I could be one of these rare happy parents, and can't see Tokai doing it either.

At the risk of being misunderstood, I would call Tokai an affable person. He wasn't a poor loser, had no inferiority complex or jealousy, no excessive biases or pride, no particular obsessions, wasn't overly sensitive, had no steadfast political views. On the surface, at least, he had none of the traits you would associate with an unstable personality. The people around him loved his straightforward, frank personality, his polished manners, and his cheerful, positive attitude. And Tokai aimed these qualities mainly at women—half of the world's population—in a strategic, effective way. Kindness and consideration for women were, for someone in his profession, necessary skills, and Tokai possessed them naturally—they were innate, inborn qualities, like a lovely voice or long fingers. Because of this (and, of course, because he was a talented surgeon), his clinic did a booming business. He never advertised, yet his appointment schedule was always full.

As my readers are no doubt aware, affable people like this are most often shallow, mediocre, and boring. Tokai, though, exhibited none of these qualities. I always enjoyed kicking back for an hour on weekends with him, having a couple of beers. He was an excellent conversationalist, with a wealth of topics. His sense of humor was always straightforward, never especially complex. He told me many interesting behind-the-scenes plastic surgery tales (always, of course, protecting the clients' privacy), and he disclosed a number of fascinating facts about women. Never once, though, did he let these descend into vulgarity. He always spoke of his women friends with great respect and affection, and took care to keep any personal information secret.

"A gentleman doesn't talk much about the taxes he paid, or the women he sleeps with," he told me once.

"Who said that?" I asked.

"I made it up," he said, his expression unchanged. "Of course, sometimes I do have to talk about taxes with my accountant."

Tokai never found it odd to have two or three girlfriends simultaneously. The women were either married or had other boyfriends, so their schedules took precedence, which cut into the time he could spend with them. He felt that having several girlfriends was only natural, and never saw it as an act of infidelity. Still, he never told any of them about the others, instead retaining a strict need-to-know policy.

At Tokai's clinic he had an accomplished male secretary who had worked for him for years. This man coordinated Tokai's complicated schedule like a veteran air traffic controller. Not only did he arrange Tokai's work schedule but, over time, the secretary had inherited the task of managing Tokai's personal dating schedule. He knew every colorful detail of Tokai's private life but never spoke about it, never looked upset about being kept so busy, and went about his work efficiently. He was good at traffic control, so Tokai wasn't involved in any near disasters. It's a little hard to believe at first, but he even kept track of his girlfriends' menstrual schedules. When

Tokai traveled with a woman, his secretary secured train tickets and hotel reservations. Without this able secretary Tokai's refined personal life would not have been the same. To thank him for all he did, Tokai made sure to give this handsome secretary (who was, of course, gay) gifts whenever the occasion warranted it.

Fortunately, the husbands and lovers of his girlfriends never once discovered Tokai's relationship with them, so he'd never experienced any major problems, nor was he put in awkward situations. He was a cautious, careful person and he warned his girlfriends to be equally discrete. He issues three key pieces of advice: take your time and don't force things; don't fall into predictable patterns; and when you do have to lie, make sure to keep it simple. (This was, of course, like trying to teach a seagull how to fly, but he made sure of it, just the same.)

Not that things were completely trouble free. Balancing so many simultaneous relationships over that length of time meant there were bound to be problems. Even a monkey misses the occasional branch and falls. One of his girlfriends gave her suspicious boyfriend reason to phone the clinic and demand to know about the doctor's personal life, as well as his morals. (His adroit secretary used his powers of persuasion to deflect the man's accusations.) And there was one married woman who got a little too wrapped up in their relationship, became unmoored, and caused some trouble for Tokai. The woman's husband happened to be a famous wrestler. But here, too, trouble was averted. The doctor managed to avoid having his shoulder broken.

"Weren't you just lucky?" I asked.

"Probably," he said, and smiled. "I probably was just

lucky. But I don't think that's all it was. By no stretch of the imagination am I all that bright, but sometimes I'm surprised by how smart I can be."

"Smart," I repeated.

"It's like—how should I put it?—my brain suddenly turns on when things get delicate . . . ," Tokai stammered. He didn't seem to be able to come up with a good example. Or perhaps he was just hesitant to discuss it.

"Speaking of being quick on the draw," I said, "I remember a scene from an old François Truffaut film. A woman says to a man, 'Some people are polite, and some are quick. Each one's a good quality to have, but most of the time quickness trumps politeness.' Have you ever seen that film?"

"No, I don't think so," Tokai said.

"The woman gave an example. A man opens a door to find a woman inside naked, changing her clothes. The polite person says, 'Excuse me, madam,' and swiftly shuts the door. The one who says 'Excuse me, monsieur' and shuts the door, now that's somebody who's quick."

"I see," Tokai said, sounding impressed. "That's an interesting definition. I think I know what they're getting at. I've been in that kind of situation a number of times."

"And each time you were able to use your mental agility to extract yourself?"

Tokai gave me a sour look. "I don't want to overestimate myself. Basically I've been lucky. I'm simply a polite, lucky man. That might be the best way to think of it."

At any rate, Tokai's so-called lucky life continued for some thirty years. A long time, when you think about it.

But one day, quite unexpectedly, he fell deeply in love. Like a clever fox suddenly finds itself caught in a trap.

The woman he fell in love with was sixteen years his junior, and married. Her husband, two years her senior, worked for a foreign IT corporation, and they had one child. A five-year-old girl. She and Tokai had been seeing each other for a year and a half.

"Mr. Tanimura," he asked me one time, "have you ever tried really hard not to love somebody too much?" This was the beginning of summer, as I recall, over a year since we first got to know each other.

"I don't think I have," I told him.

"Neither have I. Until now," Tokai said.

"Trying really hard not to love somebody too much?"

"Exactly. That's what I'm doing right now."

"Why?"

"It's simple, really. If I love her too much, it's painful. I can't take it. I don't think my heart can stand it, which is why I'm trying not to fall in love with her."

He seemed totally serious. His expression lacked any trace of his usual humor.

"What are you doing, exactly, so that you don't love her too much?"

"I've tried all kinds of things," he said. "But it all boils down to intentionally thinking negative thoughts about her as much as I can. I mentally list as many of her defects as I can come up with—her *imperfections*, I should say. And I repeat these over and over in my head like a mantra, convincing myself not to love this woman more than I should."

"Has it worked?"

"No, not so well." Tokai shook his head. "First of all, I couldn't come up with many negative things about her. And there's the fact that I find even those negative qualities attractive. And another thing is I can't tell myself what's too much for me, and what isn't. This is the first time in my life I've ever had these kind of senseless feelings."

"You've gone out with so many women and you've never been this worked up before?" I asked.

"This is the first time," the doctor said simply. Then he dragged out an old memory from deep within. "You know, there was a short period, actually, back in high school, when I felt something similar. A time when thinking about a certain person made my chest ache and I couldn't think of anything else . . . But this was a one-sided feeling that didn't go anywhere. Things are different now. I'm an adult, and we actually have a physical relationship. Even so, my mind's a total mess. The more I think about her, the more it's actually affecting me physically, my internal organs. Especially my digestive and respiratory systems."

He was silent, as if checking both systems.

"From what you're telling me," I said, "it sounds like you're trying your best not to fall too deeply for her, but also hoping not to lose her."

"Exactly. It's contradictory, I know. Schizophrenic. I'm hoping for two completely opposite things at the same time. That's not going to work out, no matter how hard I try. But I can't help it. I just can't lose her. If that happened, I'd lose myself."

"But she's married, and has a child."

"Correct."

"How does she see your relationship?"

Tokai inclined his head and carefully chose his words. "I'm just guessing, and guessing makes me even more confused. But she's told me quite clearly that she has no intention of divorcing her husband. There's the child to consider, and she doesn't want to break up their family."

"Yet she keeps on seeing you."

"We're still trying to find opportunities to see each other. But who knows about the future. She's afraid that her husband will find out about us, and she said she may stop seeing me someday. And maybe he *will* find out and we really will have to stop seeing each other. Or maybe she'll simply get tired of our affair. I have no idea what tomorrow will bring."

"And that's what frightens you the most."

"Yes, when I think about those possibilities, I can't think of anything else. I can barely even eat."

Dr. Tokai and I got to know each other at a gym near my house. He always went to the gym on weekend mornings to play squash and we ended up playing a few games together. He was a good opponent—polite, in good shape, and not overly worried about winning, and I enjoyed playing against him. I was slightly older, but we were basically the same generation (this all took place a while ago) and had roughly the same level of ability when it came to squash. We'd get all sweaty chasing the ball around, then head out to a nearby beer hall to have a few pints together. As with most people who are well raised, well educated, and financially secure, Dr. Tokai only thought of himself. But in spite of all this, as previously mentioned, he was a wonderful conversationalist and I really enjoyed talking with him.

When he found out I was a writer he gradually began to reveal more personal details. He may have felt that, like therapists and religious leaders, writers had a legitimate right (or duty) to hear people's confessions. I've had the same experience with many other people. Nevertheless, I've always enjoyed listening, and I never lost interest in what he had to tell me. He was open and honest and self-reflective. And he wasn't all that afraid of revealing his weaknesses to others—an unusual quality.

This is what he told me. "I've been out with lots of woman who are much prettier than her, better built, with better taste, and more intelligent. But those comparisons are meaningless. Because to me she is someone special. A 'complete presence,' I guess you could call it. All of her qualities are tightly bound into one core. You can't separate each individual quality to measure and analyze it, to say it's better or worse than the same quality in someone else. It's what's in her core that attracts me so strongly. Like a powerful magnet. It's beyond logic."

We were drinking some large Black and Tans while munching on fried potatoes and pickles.

"'Having seen my love now / and said farewell / I know how very shallow my heart was of old / as if I had never before known love,'" Tokai intoned.

"Gonchunagon Atsutada's poem," I said. I had no idea why I remembered this.

"In college," he said, "they taught us that '*seen*' meant

a lover's tryst, including a physical relationship. At the time it didn't mean much, but now, at this age, I've finally experienced what the poet felt. The deep sense of loss after you've met the woman you love, have made love, then said goodbye. Like you're suffocating. The same emotion hasn't changed at all in a thousand years. I've never had this feeling up till now, and it makes me realize how incomplete I've been, as a person. I was a little late in noticing this, though."

With something like that there's no such thing as too soon or too late, I told him. Your understanding may have come a little late in life, but that's better than never realizing it at all.

"But maybe it would have been better if I'd experienced this while I was still young," Tokai said. "Then I would have developed love antibodies."

I didn't think things were that simple. I knew a few people who, far from developing love antibodies, carried around a dormant but vicious disease. But I didn't bring this up. It would have taken too long to get into.

"I've been seeing her for a year and a half," he said. "Her husband often goes on business trips abroad, and when he's away we get together, have dinner, go to my place, and sleep together. She started the relationship with me when she found out her husband was having an affair. Her husband apologized to her, left the other woman, and promised he'd never do it again. But that didn't satisfy her, and she started sleeping with me to regain her emotional balance. Revenge is a strong word, but she had some mental adjustment she had to do. It happens a lot."

I wasn't sure whether this kind of thing happened a lot or not. So I kept quiet and heard him out.

"We really enjoyed ourselves. Sparkling conversation,

intimate secrets only the two of us knew, and leisurely, sensitive sex. I think we shared some beautiful times together. She laughed a lot. She has an infectious laugh. But as our relationship progressed, I fell deeply in love with her, and I couldn't turn back. And recently I've often started to wonder: Who in the world am I?"

I felt like I hadn't quite heard (or perhaps had misheard) these last words, so I asked him to repeat them.

"Who in the world am I? I've really been wondering about this," he repeated.

"That's a difficult question," I said.

"It is. A very difficult question," Tokai said. He nodded a couple of times, as if confirming this. He seemed to have missed the hint of sarcasm in my words.

"Who am I?" he went on. "Up until now I've worked as a cosmetic plastic surgeon and never had any doubts about it. Graduated from the plastic surgery department of med school, worked first with my father as his assistant, then took over the clinic when his eyes started to go and he retired. Maybe I shouldn't say this, but I'm a pretty skilled surgeon. The world of plastic surgery can be pretty seedy, and there are some clinics that put out splashy advertising but do mediocre work. I've always been conscientious about my work, and I've never had any major problems with my clients. I'm proud of this, as a professional. I'm happy with my private life, too. I have a lot of friends, and have stayed healthy up till now. I'm enjoying life. But still these days I've often wondered, Who in the world am I? And very seriously at that. If you took away my career as a plastic surgeon, and the happy environment I'm living in, and threw me out into the world, with no explanation, and with everything stripped away—what in the world would I be?"

Tokai looked me right in the eye, as if seeking some sort of response.

"Why have you suddenly started to think that way?" I asked.

"I think it's because of a book I read a while ago about the Nazi concentration camps. There was a story about a doctor of internal medicine who was sent to Auschwitz during the war. He was Jewish and had his own clinic in Berlin, but one day he and his whole family were suddenly arrested and shipped off to Auschwitz. Up till then, he'd been loved by his family, respected by those around him, trusted by his patients. He'd lived a full life in an elegant home. He had a couple of dogs, and on weekends he played cello in an amateur chamber music group of friends—mostly Schubert and Mendelssohn. His life was peaceful and full. But then, in an instant, he was thrown into a living hell. No longer was he the affluent Berliner, the respected doctor—suddenly he was barely human. He was separated from his family and treated no better than a stray dog, barely getting anything to eat. The camp commandant learned he was a well-known doctor and kept him out of the gas chambers for the time being, figuring he might be of some use, but he had no idea what the next day might bring. He might at any time, on the whim of the guards, be bludgeoned to death with a truncheon. By this time the rest of his family had probably been murdered already."

He paused for a moment.

"When I read this, it shocked me. If the time and place had been different, I might very well have suffered the same terrible fate. If for some reason—I don't know why—I was suddenly dragged away from my present life, deprived of all my rights, and reduced to living as a number, what in the world would I become? I shut the book and thought about this. Other than my skills as a plastic surgeon, and the trust I've earned from others, I have no other redeeming features, no other talents. I'm just a fifty-two-year-old man. I'm healthy, though I don't have the stamina I had when I was young. I wouldn't be able to stand hard physical labor for long. The things I'm good at are selecting a nice Pinot Noir, frequenting some sushi restaurants and others where I'm considered a valued customer, choosing stylish accessories as gifts for women, playing the piano a little (I can sight-read simple sheet music). But that's about the size of it. If I were thrown into a place like Auschwitz, none of that would help."

I agreed with him. In a concentration camp Pinot Noir, amateur piano performances, and sparkling conversational skills would be totally useless.

"Have you ever thought that way, Mr. Tanimura? What you would be if the ability to write was taken away from you?"

I explained my stance to him. My starting point was being a simple person with nothing, starting life as if stripped bare. Through chance I happened to start writing and, luckily, was able to make a living at it. So I don't need to come up with some dramatic scenario like being thrown into Auschwitz, I told him, to realize that I'm just a human being with no special qualities or skills.

Tokai mulled this over. It seemed like the first time he'd ever heard that such a point of view even existed.

"I see," he said. "That might make life a little easier."

I pointed out, hesitantly, that starting out life as a pared-down human with nothing might not, after all, be that easy.

"You're right," Tokai said. "You're absolutely right. Starting life with nothing must be hard. In that sense, I'm more blessed than most. Still, when you get to a certain age, and have created your own lifestyle and social standing, and only then start having grave doubts about your value as a human being, that becomes pretty trying too, in a different sense. The life I've lived till now seems pointless, a waste. If I were younger it'd be possible to change, and I'd still have hope. But at my age the past weighs me down. It's not so easy to start over."

"And you started to seriously think about these things after reading the book about the Nazi concentration camps?" I asked.

"Yes. The book shocked me. On top of this, it was unclear what future this woman and I have, and the combination gave me a mild case of middle-aged depression. *Who in the world am I?* I've been incessantly asking myself this. But no matter how much I ask, I can't find an answer. I just keep going around in circles. Things that I used to enjoy I now find boring. I don't feel like exercising, or buying clothes. It's too much trouble to sit down at the piano anymore. I don't even feel much like eating. I just sit there and think about her. Even when I'm with a client, my mind's full of her. I'm afraid I might even blurt out her name."

"How often do you see her?"

"It's always different, and depends on her husband's schedule. That's one of the things that's so hard for me. When he's off on a long business trip, we can see each other a lot. Her parents look after her child, or else she hires a babysitter. But when her husband's in Japan, weeks can go by without us seeing each other. Those times are awful. It's a cliché, I know, but when I think I might never see her again, I feel like I'm being torn in two."

I listened to him without comment. His choice of words, though trite, didn't strike me as clichéd. In fact, it sounded pretty real.

He took a long, slow breath, then exhaled. "I usually have multiple girlfriends. You might be startled to hear this, but sometimes as many as four or five at a time. When I can't see one, I see another, which makes things pretty easy. But once I found myself so attracted to this particular woman, the other women no longer do a thing for me. When I'm with somebody else, I see only her face. I can't get rid of it. This is a serious case."

A serious case, I thought. I pictured Tokai calling for an ambulance. "Hello? We need an ambulance here right away. This is a really serious case. Trouble breathing, feels like I'm about to be ripped apart . . ."

"One huge problem is that the more I get to know her, the more I love her. We've gone out for a year and a half, but right now I'm even more entranced than I was at the beginning. It feels like our hearts have become intertwined. Like when she feels something, my heart moves in tandem. Like we're two boats tied together with rope. Even if you want to cut the rope, there's no knife sharp enough to do it. I've never experienced this—ever. And it scares me. If my feelings for her get even stronger, what in the world's going to happen to me?"

"I see," I said. Tokai seemed to be hoping for a more substantive response.

"Mr. Tanimura, what should I do?"

"I don't have any practical suggestions," I said, "but

from what you tell me, what you're feeling now seems normal and understandable. Falling in love is like that. You can't control your feelings, and it's like some outrageous power is manipulating you. What you're going through is nothing abnormal. You've just fallen deeply in love with a woman, and you don't want to lose her. You want to keep on seeing her. If you can't, then it feels like the end of the world. This is natural. Nothing strange or unusual about it. Just one aspect of a perfectly normal life."

Dr. Tokai sat there with his arms folded. He didn't seem convinced. He may have had trouble grasping the concept of "one aspect of a perfectly normal life."

We finished our beers and were about to leave when— as though he were about to make a secret confession—he said, "Mr. Tanimura, what scares me the most, and makes me the most confused, is the rage I feel inside me."

"Rage?" I asked, surprised. Rage seemed the most unlikely emotion a person like Tokai would ever have. "Rage at what?"

Tokai shook his head. "I don't know. Definitely not rage directed at her. But when I haven't seen her for a while, when I can't see her, I feel that rage welling up. I can't grasp, though, what it's about. But it's the most intense anger I've ever felt before. It's like I want to toss everything in the apartment out the window. Chairs, TV, books, dishes, framed pictures, you name it. I don't care if they hit a pedestrian below on the head and kill him. It's ridiculous, but that's how I feel in the moment. I can control this rage, for the time being. I'm not about to really do any of that. But the day might come when I can't control myself anymore. And I might hurt someone. That's what terrifies me. If that's what's going to happen, I'd rather hurt myself."

I don't recall what I said to him. No doubt some non-committal words of consolation. Because at the time I couldn't really understand what this "rage" he spoke of meant or suggested. I should have said something more helpful. But even if I had, his fate probably wouldn't have been any different. I believe this.

We paid the bill, left the bar, and each returned home. He climbed into a cab, racket bag in hand, and waved to me from inside. This was the last time I ever saw Dr. Tokai. It was near the end of September, when the summer heat still lingered.

After that, Tokai didn't show up at the gym. I went to the gym on the weekends, hoping to run across him then, but he was never there. No one had heard anything. But that often happens at gyms. People who are regulars suddenly stop coming. The gym isn't a workplace. People are free to come and go as they please. So I didn't worry about it much. Two months passed.

On a Friday afternoon at the end of November, Tokai's secretary called me. His name was Goto. His voice was low and smooth and reminded me of Barry White's music. The kind they play on late-night FM programs.

"It's painful for me to have to tell you this over the phone," he said, "but Dr. Tokai passed away last Thursday. On Monday of this week his family held a private funeral for him."

"Passed away?" I said, dumbfounded. "He was fine when I last saw him two months ago. What happened?"

Goto was silent. Finally, he said, "I can't really go into it over the phone. Actually, while he was still alive, Dr. Tokai entrusted me with something he wanted to give to you. I'm sorry to bother you, but could we get together for a while? I'll tell you all about it then. I can meet at any time, anywhere."

How about today, right after this? I asked. That would be fine, Goto replied. I named a cafeteria on a backstreet one street off Aoyama Boulevard. Let's meet at six, I told him. We should be able to have a quiet talk there. Goto didn't know the place, but said he'd be able to find it.

When I showed up at the cafeteria at five minutes till six, Goto was already seated, and as I approached he quickly got to his feet. From the low voice on the phone I was expecting some powerfully built man, but in reality he was tall and slim. He was, as Tokai had once told me, quite handsome. Goto had on a brown wool suit, white button-down shirt, and dark mustard-colored tie. A perfect outfit. His longish hair was neat, forelocks pleasantly falling on his forehead. He looked to be in his mid-thirties, and if I hadn't heard from Tokai that he was gay, I would have taken him for just a traditional, well-dressed young man. (I say "young" because he still looked quite youthful.) He looked like he had a thick beard. He was drinking a double espresso.

We exchanged a quick greeting, and I ordered the same.

"He passed away so suddenly, didn't he?" I asked.

The young man narrowed his eyes, as if he were facing into a bright light. "Yes, his death was quite sudden. Surprisingly so. Yet it also took a long time, and was a painful way to die."

I didn't say anything, waiting for him to explain. But

he didn't seem to want to give any of the details of the doctor's death—at least not until the waiter brought my drink.

"I respected Dr. Tokai very much," the young man said, as if changing the subject. "He was truly a wonderful person, as a doctor, and as a human being. He taught me all kinds of things, and was always patient and kind. I worked at the clinic for nearly ten years, and if I hadn't met him, I wouldn't be the person I am today. He was straightforward, decent. Always upbeat, never arrogant. He treated people fairly and cared about everyone. They all liked him. I never heard him, not even once, say something bad about someone else."

Come to think of it, I'd never heard him bad-mouth anyone either.

"Dr. Tokai spoke very highly of you, too," I said. "He said that without you he couldn't run the clinic, and that his private life would be a complete mess."

A faint, sad smile rose to Goto's lips. "I'm not as good as all that. I just wanted to work behind the scenes, as hard as I could, to help him. And I enjoyed it."

The waitress brought over my espresso, and after she left he finally began to talk about the doctor's death.

"The first thing I noticed was that he stopped eating lunch. Before that he always ate something, every day, even something simple. He was very particular about making sure he ate, no matter how busy work was. But at a certain point he stopped eating lunch altogether. 'Won't you have something?' I'd urge him, and he'd say, 'Don't worry, I'm just not hungry.' This was at the beginning of October. This change concerned me. He was not the kind of person who liked to alter his day-today habits. He valued regularity above all. Before I realized it, he stopped going to the gym, too. He always went three times a week to swim, play squash, and do strength training, but suddenly he seemed to have lost interest. And he stopped paying attention to his appearance. He'd always been a neat, stylish man, but he became a sloppy dresser. He started wearing the same clothes day after day. And he seemed lost in thought and grew quiet. At a certain point, he hardly said a word, and half the time it was as though he was in a daze. When I spoke to him he didn't seem to hear me. And he stopped seeing women in his free time."

"You kept his schedule, so I imagine you witnessed those changes quite clearly?"

"That's true. Seeing his lady friends was an important daily event. The source of his energy. Cutting them out all of sudden wasn't normal. Fifty-two isn't too old for that. I'm sure you knew, Mr. Tanimura, about how active Dr. Tokai was when it came to women in his life?"

"He didn't particularly keep it secret. He never bragged about it, but was always pretty open, is what I mean."

Goto nodded. "He told me all kinds of things, too. Which is why this sudden change came as such a shock. He kept it all to himself and never revealed anything to me about it. Of course I asked him if something had gone wrong, or if there was something that was worrying him, but he just shook his head and didn't elaborate. By this point he was barely speaking to me. He was visibly getting thinner and weaker every day. Clearly he wasn't eating enough. But I couldn't intrude on his private life. He was a very candid person, but past a certain point, he valued his privacy. In all the years I'd worked as his personal secretary, I'd only been to his home once, to pick up something important he'd forgotten. Probably only the women he saw were allowed to visit him at home. So I could only speculate and worry from a distance."

Goto let out a small sigh, as if resigned to the fact that these women Tokai was intimate with had access that he had not been granted.

"He got thinner and weaker by the day?" I asked.

"Correct. His eyes grew sunken, his face was pale like paper. He couldn't walk steadily and wasn't able to use a scalpel anymore. There was no way he could operate on patients. Fortunately, he had an excellent assistant who temporarily took over the surgeries. But things couldn't go on like that indefinitely. I called around, canceling all his appointments, and the clinic was, for all intents and purposes, closed. Finally, he stopped showing up at the clinic altogether. This was at the end of October. I called him, but no one answered. I couldn't reach him for two whole days. I had a key to his apartment, and on the morning of the third day, I took the key and let myself inside. I know I shouldn't have, but I was getting frantic with worry.

"When I opened the door I was hit with a horrible smell. The floor was littered with all kinds of things—clothes scattered all over, suits, neckties, underwear. It looked like no one had cleaned up in months. The windows were closed, and the air was stifling. I found him on the bed, just quietly lying there."

Goto closed his eyes and shook his head. He seemed to be recalling the scene.

"When I saw him, I was sure he was dead. My heart felt like it was going to stop. But he wasn't dead. He turned his gaunt, pale face in my direction, opened his eyes, and looked at me. He blinked a few times. He was breathing, though faintly. He just lay there, unmoving, the covers pulled up to his neck. I spoke to him but got no reaction. His dry lips were closed tight, like they were sewn shut. He hadn't shaved for a long time. I opened up the windows to let in some fresh air. It didn't seem to me that I needed to take any immediate emergency action, and he didn't seem to be in pain, so I went ahead and straightened up the apartment. The place was a complete disaster. I gathered up the scattered clothes, washed what I could in the washing machine, put what needed to be dry-cleaned in a bag to take to the store. I drained the stagnant bathwater and scrubbed the dirty ring from the inside of the tub. Dr. Tokai had always been so neat, and I found this mess impossible to fathom. The furniture was covered in white dust, and it seemed he'd stopped having the cleaning woman come in. Strangely enough, there were hardly any dirty dishes piled up in the kitchen sink. It alone was clean. He obviously hadn't used the kitchen in some time. There were a couple of empty mineral water bottles around, but no sign that he'd eaten anything. I opened the fridge and there was this indescribably awful stink. The food left inside had all spoiled. Tofu, vegetables, fruit, milk, sandwiches, ham, and the like. I packed them all in a big plastic garbage bag and took it to the garbage area outside the apartment building."

Goto lifted his empty espresso cup and studied it from a variety of angles. He finally looked up.

"It took over three hours to get the apartment back to the way it should be. I left the windows open the whole time so that by the time I was finished, the stench was nearly gone. But Dr. Tokai hadn't said a word the whole time. He just followed me with his eyes as I moved about the room. He was so gaunt that his eyes looked bigger and shinier than usual. But I couldn't detect any emotion in them. They were watching me but not really seeing anything. I'm not sure how to put it. They were simply following the movements of some *object*, like an automatic camera lens focusing in on a moving target. It was like he didn't care that it was me, or couldn't be bothered to notice what I was doing. His eyes were so sad. I'll never forget them as long as I live.

"I used an electric razor, shaved him, and wiped his face with a damp towel. He didn't resist at all. He just let me do whatever I wanted. After this I phoned his personal physician. When I explained the situation, the doctor came right over. He examined him and conducted a few simple tests. Dr. Tokai never said a word. He just stared at our faces with those impassive, vacant eyes the whole time.

"This might not be the right way of putting it, but he no longer looked like a living person. It was like he'd been buried in the ground, and should have turned into a mummy because he had no food. But, of course, he was unable give up worldly attachments, and unable to become a mummy, so he'd crawled back out onto the surface. That's what it was like. I know it's an awful way to put it, but that's exactly how I felt. He'd lost his soul, and it wasn't coming back. But his bodily organs, unable to give up, continued to function independently. That's what it felt like."

The young man shook his head a few times.

"I'm sorry I've taken so long to tell you this. I'll finish up. Dr. Tokai was basically suffering from something like anorexia. He'd hardly been eating a thing, and had remained alive only because he was drinking water. Strictly speaking, it wasn't anorexia. As I'm sure you know, it's almost always young women who get anorexia. They cut back on calories so they can look good and lose weight, and soon losing weight itself becomes its own goal and they end up starving themselves. In extreme cases these women hope to reduce their weight to nothing. So even though it's unthinkable that a middle-aged man would become ill with anorexia, in Dr. Tokai's case that's exactly what had happened. Of course, this had nothing to do with wanting to appear more attractive. I think he *literally* could not manage to swallow any more food."

"Because he was lovesick?" I asked.

"Something close to that," Goto said. "Or else a similar desire to reduce himself to nothing. Maybe he wanted to erase himself. Otherwise a normal person couldn't stand the pain of starvation like that. Perhaps the joy of the body shrinking to nothing won out over the pain. Just like what women with anorexia must feel as they watch their bodies shrink away."

I tried picturing Dr. Tokai lying in bed, obsessed by love to the point where he became a shriveled mummy. But all I could imagine was the person I knew, a cheerful, healthy, well-dressed man who loved good food.

"The doctor gave him nutritional shots and brought in a nurse to monitor an IV. But nutritional injections can only do so much, and if the patient wants to remove the IV, he can. And I couldn't stay by his bedside night and day. I could have forced him to eat something, but then he would have just vomited it up. If a person is opposed to being hospitalized, you can't very well force it on them. At this point Dr. Tokai had given up the will to live and decided to reduce himself to nothing. No matter what anybody did, no matter how many nutritional injections we gave him, there was no stopping this downward progression. All we could do was stand by, arms folded, and watch as starvation devoured his body. These were painful, trying days. I knew I should do something, but there was nothing to be done. The sole saving grace was that he didn't seem to be in any pain. At least I never saw him wince. I went to his apartment every day, checked his mail, cleaned, and sat next to his bed, talking to him about all kinds of things. News related to work, gossip. But he never said a word. Never showed anything close to a reaction. I'm not even sure he was conscious. He just silently stared at me with his big eyes, his face like a mask. Those eyes were oddly clear. As if they could see to the other side."

"Did something happen between him and a woman?" I asked. "He told me how serious he was getting about a married woman who had a child."

"That's right. From some time before this, he had gotten deeply involved with her. It was no longer a casual affair. Something very serious had happened between the two of them, and whatever it was caused him to lose the will to live. I tried phoning that woman's home. Her husband answered. I told him I needed to talk with her about an appointment she'd made at our clinic, but he said she no longer lived there. Where should I phone to get in touch with her? I asked, and he said, very coldly, that he had no idea. And he hung up."

He was silent for a while, then went on.

"Long story short, I was able to track her down. She had left her husband and child, and was living with another man."

I was speechless. At first I couldn't grasp what he was getting at. "You're saying she walked out on both her husband and Dr. Tokai?" I finally managed to ask.

"Yes," Goto said. He frowned. "She had a third man. I don't know all the particulars, but he seems to have been younger than her. This is just my own opinion, but I got the sense that he wasn't exactly the kind of man you'd admire. She'd run away from home to elope with him. Dr. Tokai turned out to be just a convenient stepping stone and nothing more. She used him. There's evidence he spent quite a lot of money on her. I got lawyers involved and they checked his bank balances and credit card accounts, and this became clear. He probably spent all that money buying expensive gifts for her. Or maybe he loaned her money. There's no clear evidence that shows exactly how the funds were used, and the details remain unclear, but what we know is that he withdrew a significant amount of money over a short period of time."

I sighed heavily. "That must have been hard on him."

The young man nodded. "If that woman had told him 'I decided I can't leave my husband and child, so I have to break up with you,' then I think he could have stood it. He loved her more than he had ever loved anybody before, so of course he would have been devastated, but I doubt it would have driven him to death. As long as it all makes sense, no matter how deep you fall, you should be able to pull yourself together again. But the appearance of a third man, and the realization that he'd been used, was a shock he couldn't recover from."

I listened silently.

"When he died, Dr. Tokai weighed less than eighty pounds," the young man said. "Normally he weighed over one sixty, so he was under half his normal weight. His ribs stuck out like rocks when the tide goes out. You didn't want to look at him, it was so awful. It made me think of the emaciated Jewish survivors of Nazi concentration camps that I saw in a documentary a long time ago."

Concentration camps. In a sense he'd foreseen this. *Who in the world* am *I? I've really been wondering about this.*

Goto went on. "Medically speaking, the direct cause of death was heart failure. His heart lost the strength to pump blood. But I think his death was brought on because he was in love. To use the old term, he was indeed 'lovesick.' I phoned the woman many times, explaining what was going on and asking her to help. I literally went down on my knees, pleading with her to come see him, even for a little while. At this point, I told her, he's going to die. But she never came. Of course, I didn't think that just seeing her was going to keep him from dying. Dr. Tokai had already made up his mind to die. But maybe a miracle would have taken place. Or else he would have had different feelings as he died. Or maybe seeing her would have only confused him, and caused him more pain. I don't really know. Truthfully, I didn't understand any of it. There's one thing I do know, however. Nobody's ever stopped eating completely and actually died just from being lovesick. Don't you think so?"

I agreed. I'd never heard of such a thing. In that sense, Dr. Tokai was a special person. When I said this, Goto covered his face with his hands and silently cried for a while. He truly loved Dr. Tokai. I wanted to console him, but there was nothing I could do. After a while he stopped crying, took out a clean white handkerchief from his pants pocket, and wiped away the tears.

"I'm sorry you had to see me like this."

"Crying for someone else is nothing to apologize about," I told him. "Especially someone you care for, someone who's passed away."

"Thank you," Goto said. "It helps to hear that."

He reached under the table for the squash racket case and passed it to me. Inside was a brand-new Black Knight racket. An expensive one.

"Dr. Tokai left this with me. He'd ordered it through the mail, but by the time it arrived he didn't have the strength to play squash anymore. He asked me to give it to you, Mr. Tanimura. Just before he died he was fully conscious for a short time and he gave me some instructions, things he wanted me to take care of. This racket was one of them. Please use it if you'd like."

I thanked him and took the racket. "What's going to happen to the clinic?" I asked.

"We'll stay closed for the time being," he said. "We'll either close the clinic, eventually, or put it up for sale. There's still office work to do, so I'll be helping out for a while, but I haven't decided about after that. I need to have a sense of closure, but right now I'm just not thinking straight."

I hoped very much that this young man would recover from the shock.

As we were saying goodbye he said, "Mr. Tanimura, I know this is an imposition, but I have a favor to ask. Please remember Dr. Tokai. He had such a pure heart. I think that what we can do for those who've passed on is keep them in our memories as long as we can. But it's not as easy as it sounds. I can't ask just anyone to do that."

You're absolutely right, I told him. Remembering someone for a long time is not as easy as people think. I'll try to remember him as long as I can, I promised. I had no way to decide how pure Dr. Tokai's heart really was, but it was true that he was no ordinary person, and certainly someone worth remembering. We shook hands and said goodbye.

I suppose that's why I'm writing this account—in order not to forget Dr. Tokai. For me, writing things down is an effective method of not forgetting. I've changed the names and places slightly so as not to cause any trouble, but all the events actually took place, pretty much as I've related them. It would be nice if young Goto happened across this account and read it.

There's one other thing I remember very well about Dr. Tokai. I can't recall how we got on to the topic, but he was chatting to me about women in general.

Women are all born with a special, independent organ that allows them to lie. This was Dr. Tokai's personal opinion. It depends on the person, he said, about the kind of lies they tell, what situation they tell them in, and how the lies are told. But at a certain point in their lives, all women tell lies, and they lie about important things. They lie about unimportant things, too, but they also don't hesitate to lie about the most important things. And when they do, most women's expressions and voices don't change at all, since it's not them lying, but this independent organ they're equipped with that's acting on its own. That's why—except in a few special cases—they can still have a clear conscience and never lose sleep over anything they say.

He said all this very decisively, which is why I remember it so well. I basically have to agree with him, though the specific nuances in what he was saying may be a bit different. He and I may have arrived at the same not-so-pleasant summit, even though we'd climbed there on our own.

I'm sure that, as he faced death, he got no joy in the confirmation that this theory was correct. Needless to say, I feel very sorry for Dr. Tokai. I truly mourn his death. It took great fortitude to deliberately stop eating and starve himself to death. The physical and emotional pain he must have suffered is beyond comprehension. But I don't mind admitting that I'm a little envious of the way he loved one woman—putting aside what sort of woman she was—so deeply that it made him want to reduce himself to nothing. If he'd wanted to, he could have continued and carried out his contrived life as before. Casually seeing several women at the same time, enjoying a glass of a mellow Pinot Noir, playing "My Way" on the grand piano in his living room, enjoying some happy little love affairs in a corner of the city. But he fell so desperately, hopelessly in love that he could no longer even eat, that he stepped into a completely new world, saw things he'd never before witnessed, and eventually drove himself to death. As Goto put it, he was *erasing* himself. I couldn't say which of these two lives was truly happy and real for him. The fate that followed Dr. Tokai from September to November of that year was full of mysteries that I, just like Goto, simply could not fathom.

I still play squash, but after Dr. Tokai died I moved and, as a result, changed gyms. In the new gym I generally play with hired partners. It costs money, but it's easier. I've hardly used the racket Dr. Tokai left me. It's a bit too light. And when I feel how light it is, I can't help but picture his emaciated figure.

It feels like somehow our hearts have become intertwined. Like when she feels something, my heart moves in tandem. Like we're two boats tied together with rope. Even if you want to cut the rope, there's no knife sharp enough to do it.

Later on, of course, we all thought he'd tied himself to the wrong boat. But who can really say? Just as that woman likely lied to him with her independent organ, Dr. Tokai—in a somewhat different sense—used this independent organ to fall in love. A function beyond his will. With hindsight it's easy for someone else to sadly shake his head and smugly criticize another's actions. But without the intervention of that kind of organ—the kind that elevates us to new heights, thrusts us down to the depths, throws our minds into chaos, reveals beautiful illusions, and sometimes even drives us to death—our lives would indeed be indifferent and brusque. Or simply end up as a series of contrivances.

I have no way of knowing, of course, what Dr. Tokai thought, what sort of notions went through his head, as he teetered on the edge of his chosen death. But within the depths of his pain and suffering, if only for a short time, his mind became clear enough to leave instructions to leave me his unused squash racket. Maybe he was trying to send me some sort of message. Perhaps as he hovered near death he'd finally found something close to an answer to the question *Who am I?* And he wanted to let me know. I have a feeling that's the case.

Translated by Philip Gabriel

SCHEHERAZADE

EACH TIME THEY HAD SEX, she told Habara a strange and gripping story afterward. Like Queen Scheherazade in *A Thousand and One Nights*. Though, of course, Habara, unlike the king, had no plan to chop off her head the next morning. (She never stayed with him till morning, anyway.) She told Habara the stories because she wanted to, because, he guessed, she enjoyed curling up in bed and talking to a man during those languid, intimate moments after making love. And also, probably, because she wished to comfort Habara, who had to spend every day cooped up indoors.

Because of this, Habara had dubbed the woman Scheherazade. He never used the name to her face, but it was how he referred to her in the small diary he kept. "Scheherazade came today," he'd note in ballpoint pen. Then he'd record the gist of that day's story in simple, cryptic terms that were sure to baffle anyone who might read the diary later.

Habara didn't know whether her stories were true,

invented, or partly true and partly invented. He had no way of telling. Reality and supposition, observation and pure fancy seemed jumbled together in her narratives. Habara therefore enjoyed them as a child might, without questioning too much. What possible difference could it make to him, after all, if they were lies or truth, or a complicated patchwork of the two?

Whatever the case, Scheherazade had a gift for telling stories that touched the heart. No matter what sort of story it was, she made it special. Her voice, her timing, her pacing were all flawless. She captured her listener's attention, tantalized him, drove him to ponder and speculate, and then, in the end, gave him precisely what he'd been seeking. Enthralled, Habara was able to forget the reality that surrounded him, if only for a moment. Like a blackboard wiped with a damp cloth, he was erased of worries, of unpleasant memories. Who could ask for more? At this point in his life, that kind of forgetting was what Habara desired more than anything else.

Scheherazade was thirty-five, four years older than Habara, and a full-time housewife with two children in elementary school (though she was also a registered nurse and was apparently called in for the occasional job). Her husband was a typical company man. Their home was a twenty-minute drive away. This was all (or almost all) the personal information she had volunteered. Habara had no way of verifying any of it, but he could think of no particular reason to doubt her. She had never revealed her name. "There's no need for you to know, is there?" Scheherazade had asked. She certainly had a point. As long as they continued like this, she could remain "Scheherazade" to him—no inconvenience there.

Nor had she ever called Habara by his name, though of course she knew what it was. She judiciously steered clear of the name, as if it would somehow be unlucky or inappropriate to have it pass her lips.

On the surface, at least, this Scheherazade had nothing in common with the beautiful queen of *A Thousand and One Nights*. She was a housewife from a provincial city well on the road to middle age and running to flab (in fact it looked as if every nook and cranny had been filled with putty), with jowls and lines webbing the corners of her eyes. Her hairstyle, her makeup, and her manner of dress weren't exactly slapdash, but neither were they likely to receive any compliments. Her features were not unattractive, but her face lacked focus, so that the impression she left was somehow blurry. As a consequence, those who walked by her on the street, or shared the same elevator, probably took little notice of her. Ten years earlier, she might well have been a lively and attractive young woman, perhaps even turned a few heads. At some point, however, the curtain had fallen on that part of her life and it seemed unlikely to rise again.

Scheherazade came to see Habara twice a week. Her days were not fixed, but she never came on weekends. No doubt she spent that time with her family. She always phoned an hour before arriving. She bought groceries at the local supermarket and brought them to him in her car, a small blue Mazda hatchback. An older model, it had a dent in its rear bumper and its wheels were black with grime. Parking it in the reserved space assigned to the House, she would carry the bags to the front door and ring the bell. After checking the peephole, Habara would release the lock, unhook the chain, and let her in.

In the kitchen, she'd sort the groceries and arrange them in the refrigerator. Then she'd make a list of things to buy for her next visit. She performed these tasks skillfully, with a minimum of wasted motion, like a competent housewife, saying little throughout.

Once she'd finished, the two of them would move wordlessly to the bedroom, as if borne there by an invisible current. Scheherazade quickly removed her clothes and, still silent, joined Habara in bed. She barely spoke during their lovemaking, either, performing each act as if completing an assignment. When she was menstruating, she used her hand to accomplish the same end. Her deft, rather businesslike manner reminded Habara that she was a licensed nurse.

After sex, they lay in bed and talked. More accurately, she talked and he listened, adding an appropriate word here, asking the occasional question there. When the clock said four thirty, she would break off her story (for some reason, it always seemed to have just reached a climax), jump out of bed, gather up her clothes, and get ready to leave. She had to go home, she said, to prepare dinner.

Habara would see her to the door, replace the chain, and watch through the curtains as the grimy little blue car drove away. At six o'clock, he made a simple dinner and ate it by himself. He had once worked as a cook, so putting a meal together was no great hardship. He drank Perrier with his dinner (he never touched alcohol) and followed it with a cup of coffee, which he sipped while watching a DVD or reading. He liked long books, especially those he had to read several times to understand. There wasn't much else to do. He had no one to talk to. No one to phone. With no computer, he had no way of accessing the Internet. No newspaper was delivered, and he never watched television. (There was a good reason for that.) It went without saying that he couldn't go outside. Should Scheherazade's visits come to a halt for some reason, he would be left all alone, his ties to the outside world severed.

Habara was not overly concerned about this prospect. If that happens, he thought, it will be hard, but I'll scrape by one way or another. I'm not stranded on a desert island. No, he thought, I *am* a desert island. If he could fully grasp that concept, he could deal with whatever lay ahead. He had always been comfortable being by himself. His nerves could cope with the solitude. What did bother him, though, was the thought of not being able to talk in bed with Scheherazade. Or, more precisely, missing the next installment of her story.

Not long after settling in at the House, Habara had grown a beard. His facial hair had always been thicker than that of most other men. Of course he wanted to change his appearance, but there was more to it. The main reason was to help kill the copious amount of time he had on his hands. Once it had grown in, he could luxuriate in the sensation of stroking his beard, or his sideburns, or his mustache, for that matter. Or he could spend hours trimming his facial hair with a razor or a pair of scissors. For the first time he realized how useful a hairy face could be, simply as a diversion from boredom.

"I was a lamprey eel in a former life," Scheherazade said once, as they lay in bed together. It was a simple, straightforward comment, as offhand as if she had announced that the North Pole was in the far north. Habara hadn't a clue what sort of creature a lamprey was, much less what one looked like. So he had no particular opinion on the subject.

"Do you know how a lamprey eats a trout?" she asked.

He didn't. In fact, it was the first time he'd heard that lampreys ate trout.

"Lampreys have no jaws. That's what sets them apart from other eels."

"Huh? Eels have jaws?"

"Haven't you ever taken a good look at one?" she said, surprised.

"I do eat eel now and then, but I've never had an opportunity to see if they have jaws."

"Well, you should check it out sometime. Go to an aquarium or someplace like that. Regular eels have jaws with teeth. But lampreys have only suckers, which they use to attach themselves to rocks at the bottom of a river or lake. Then they just kind of float there, waving back and forth, like weeds."

Habara imagined a bunch of lampreys swaying like weeds at the bottom of a lake. The scene seemed somehow divorced from reality, although reality, he knew, could at times be terribly unreal.

"Lampreys live like that, hidden among the weeds. Lying in wait. Then, when a trout passes overhead, they dart up and fasten onto it with their suckers. Inside their suckers are these tongue-like things with teeth, which rub back and forth against the trout's belly until a hole opens up and they can start eating the flesh, bit by bit."

"I wouldn't like to be a trout," Habara said.

"Back in Roman times, they raised lampreys in ponds. Uppity slaves got chucked in and the lampreys ate them alive."

Habara thought that he wouldn't have enjoyed being a Roman slave, either. Of course, being a slave was a downer under any circumstances.

"The first time I saw a lamprey was back in elementary school, on a class trip to the aquarium," Scheherazade said. "The moment I read the description of how they lived, I knew that I'd been one in a former life. I mean, I could actually remember—being fastened to a rock, swaying invisibly among the weeds, eying the fat trout swimming by above me."

"Can you remember eating them?"

"No, I can't."

"That's a relief," Habara said. "But is that all you recall from your life as a lamprey—swaying to and fro at the bottom of a river?"

"A former life can't be called up just like that," she said. "If you're lucky, you can catch a flash of what it was like. It's like catching a glimpse through a tiny hole in a wall—you only get a snapshot of that little bit. Can you recall any of your former lives?"

"No, not one," Habara said. Truth be told, he had never felt the urge to revisit a former life. He had his hands full with the present one.

"Still, it felt pretty neat at the bottom of the lake. Upside down with my mouth fastened to a rock, watching the fish pass overhead. I saw a really big snapping turtle once, too, a humongous black shape drifting past, like the evil spaceship in *Star Wars*. And big white birds with long, sharp beaks that targeted the fish like gangs of assassins; from below, they looked like white clouds floating across the blue sky. We lampreys didn't have to worry about them, though—we were safe down among the weeds."

"And you can see all these things now?"

"As clear as day," Scheherazade said. "The light, the pull of the current, everything. Sometimes I can even go back there in my mind."

"To what you were thinking then?"

"Yeah."

"So you were thinking."

"Certainly."

"What do lampreys think about?"

"Lampreys think very lamprey-like thoughts. About lamprey-like topics in a context that's very lamprey-like. There are no words for those thoughts. They belong to the world of water. It's like when we were in the womb. We were thinking things in there, but we can't express those thoughts in the language we use out here. Right?"

"Hold on a second! You can remember what it was like in the womb?"

"Sure," Scheherazade said, lifting her head to see over his chest. "Can't you?"

No, he said. He couldn't.

"Then I'll tell you sometime. About life in the womb."

"Scheherazade, Lamprey, Former Lives" was what Habara recorded in his diary that day. He doubted that anyone who came across it would guess what the words meant.

Habara had met Scheherazade for the first time four months earlier. He had been transported to this House, in a provincial city north of Tokyo, and she had been assigned to him as his "support liaison." Since he couldn't go outside, her role was to buy food and other items he required and bring them to the House. She also tracked down whatever books and magazines he wished to read, and any CDs he wanted to listen to. In addition, she chose an assortment of DVDs—though he had a hard time accepting her criteria for selection on this front.

A week after he arrived, as if it were a self-evident next step, Scheherazade had taken him to bed. There had been condoms on the bedside table when he arrived. Habara guessed that sex was one of her assigned duties—or perhaps "support activities" was the term they used. Whatever the term, and whatever her motivation, he'd accepted her proposal without hesitation, allowing himself to be carried along by the flow. They went straight to bed and made love, leaving him in the dark as to the meaning of it all.

While the sex was not what you'd call passionate, it wasn't entirely businesslike, either. It may have begun as one of her duties (or, at least, as something that was strongly encouraged), but at a certain point she seemed—if only in a small way—to have found a kind of pleasure in it. Habara could tell this from certain subtle ways in which her body responded, a response that delighted him as well. After all, he was not a wild animal penned up in a cage but a human being equipped with a full range of emotions, and while sex for the sole purpose of physical release might be necessary, it was hardly fulfilling. Yet to what extent did Scheherazade see their sexual relationship as one of her duties, and how much did it belong to the sphere of her personal life? Habara found it impossible to draw a line between the two.

This was true of other things, too. Habara couldn't figure out if the everyday services she performed for him stemmed from affection—if "affection" was the right word—or if they were just part of her assignment. He often found Scheherazade's feelings and intentions hard to read. For example, she wore plain cotton panties most of the time, the kind of panties Habara imagined housewives in their thirties usually wore—though this was pure conjecture, since he had no experience with housewives of that age. The kind you could buy in bargain-basement sales. Some days, however, she turned up in really fancy, seductive panties. He didn't know where she'd picked them up, but they sure looked expensive: frilly, silky things dyed in deep colors. What purpose, what circumstances lay behind the radical difference? He sure as hell couldn't tell.

The other thing that puzzled him was the fact that their lovemaking and her storytelling were so closely linked, making it hard, if not impossible, to tell where one ended and the other began. He had never experienced anything like this before: he didn't love her, and the sex wasn't all that passionate, but he was so closely tied—one could even say sewn—to her physically. It was all rather confusing.

"I was a teenager when I started breaking into empty houses," she said one day as they lay in bed.

Habara—as was often the case when she told stories—found himself at a loss for words.

"Have you ever broken into somebody's house?" she asked.

"I don't think so," he answered in a dry voice.

"Do it once and you get addicted."

"But it's illegal."

"You bet. The police haul you in if they catch you. Breaking and entering plus robbery, or at least attempted robbery. Nothing to laugh at. You know it's dangerous but you still get hooked."

Habara waited quietly for her to continue.

"The coolest thing about being in someone else's house when no one's there," Scheherazade said, "is how silent it is. Not a sound. It's like the quietest place in the world. That's how it felt to me, anyway. When I sat on the floor and kept absolutely still, my life as a lamprey came back to me. It was so cool—it felt entirely natural. I told you about my being a lamprey in a former life, right?"

"Yes, you did."

"It was just like that. My suckers stuck to a rock underwater and my body waving back and forth overhead, like the weeds around me. Everything so quiet. Though that may have been because I had no ears. On sunny days, light shot like an arrow from the surface straight down to me. Sometimes it fractured into a sparkling prism. Fish of all colors and shapes drifted by above. And my mind was empty of thoughts. Other than lamprey thoughts, that is. Those were cloudy but very pure. Not transparent, but still without blemish. I was still myself, yet at the same time I was something different. It was a wonderful place to be."

The first time Scheherazade broke into someone's house, she explained, she was a high school junior and had a serious crush on a boy in her class. Though he wasn't what you would call handsome, he was tall and clean-cut, a good student who played on the soccer team, and she was powerfully attracted to him. Yet, as with many high school crushes, hers was a love that could never be reciprocated. He apparently liked another girl in their class and took no notice of Scheherazade. He never spoke to her—indeed, it was possible he was unaware that she even existed. Nevertheless, she couldn't get him out of her mind. Just seeing him made it hard for her to breathe; sometimes she felt as if she were going to throw up. If she didn't do something about it, she thought, she might go crazy. But confessing her love was out of the question. That was a recipe for disaster.

One day, Scheherazade skipped her morning classes and went to the boy's house. It was about a fifteen-minute walk from where she lived. She had researched his family situation beforehand. His mother taught the Japanese language at a school in a neighboring town. His father, who had worked at a cement company, had been killed in a car accident some years earlier. His sister was a junior high school student. This meant that the house should be empty during the day.

Not surprisingly, the front door was locked. Scheherazade checked under the mat for a key. Sure enough, there was one there. Quiet residential communities in provincial cities like theirs had little crime, and so people were relaxed enough to leave a spare key under a mat or a potted plant.

To be safe, Scheherazade rang the bell, waited to make sure there was no answer, scanned the street in case she was being observed, opened the door, and entered. She locked the door again from the inside. Taking off her shoes, she put them in a plastic bag and stuck it in the knapsack on her back. Then she tiptoed up the stairs to the second floor.

His bedroom was there, as she had imagined. His

small, neatly made wooden bed. A full bookshelf, a chest of drawers, and a desk. On the bookshelf was a small stereo, with a few CDs. On the wall, there was a calendar with a photo of the Barcelona soccer team and, next to it, what looked like a team banner, but nothing else. No posters, no pictures. Just a cream-colored wall. A white curtain hung over the window. The room was tidy, everything in its place. No books strewn about, no clothes on the floor. All the pens and pencils in their designated spot on the desk. The room testified to the meticulous personality of its inhabitant. Or else to a mother who kept a perfect house. Or both. It made Scheherazade nervous. Of all the luck, she thought. Had the room been sloppier, no one would have noticed whatever little messes she might make. She would have to be really careful. Yet, at the same time, the very cleanliness and simplicity of the room, its perfect order, made her happy. It was so like him.

Scheherazade lowered herself into the desk chair and sat there for a while. This is where he studies every night, she thought, her heart pounding. One by one, she picked up the implements on the desk, rolled them between her fingers, smelled them, held them to her lips. His pencils, his scissors, his ruler, his stapler, his calendar—the most mundane objects became somehow radiant by being his.

She opened his desk drawers and carefully checked their contents. The uppermost drawer was divided into compartments, each of which contained a small tray with a scattering of objects and souvenirs. The second drawer was largely occupied by notebooks for the classes he was taking at the moment, while the one on the bottom (the deepest drawer) was filled with an assortment of old papers, notebooks, and exams. Almost everything was connected either to school or to soccer. Nothing important. She'd hoped to come across something personal—a diary, perhaps, or letters—but the desk held nothing of that sort. Not even a photograph. That struck Scheherazade as a bit unnatural. Did he have no life outside of school and soccer? Or had he carefully hidden everything of a private nature, where no one would come across it?

Still, just sitting at his desk and running her eyes over his handwriting moved Scheherazade beyond words. If she didn't do something, she might lose control. To calm herself, she got out of the chair and sat on the floor. She looked up at the ceiling. The quiet around her was absolute. Not a sound anywhere. In this way, she entered the lampreys' world.

"So all you did," Habara asked, "was enter his room, go through his stuff, and sit on the floor?"

"No," Scheherazade said. "There was more. I wanted something of his to take home. Something that he handled every day or that had been close to his body. But it couldn't be anything important that he would miss. So I stole one of his pencils."

"A single pencil?"

"Yes. One that he'd been using. But stealing wasn't enough. That would make it a straightforward case of burglary. The fact that *I* had done it would be lost. I was the Love Burglar, after all."

The Love Burglar? It sounded to Habara like the title of a silent film.

"So I decided to leave something behind in its place, a token of some sort. As proof that I had been there. A declaration that this was an exchange, not a simple theft. But what should it be? Nothing popped into my head. I searched my knapsack and my pockets, but I couldn't find anything appropriate. I kicked myself for not having thought to bring something suitable. Finally, I decided to leave a tampon behind. An unused one, of course, still in its plastic wrapper. My period was getting close, so I was carrying it around just to be safe. I hid it at the very back of the bottom drawer, where it would be difficult to find. That really turned me on. The fact that a tampon of mine was stashed away in his desk drawer. Maybe it was because I was so turned on that my period started almost immediately after that."

A tampon for a pencil, Habara thought. Perhaps that was what he should write in his diary that day: "Love Thief, Pencil, Tampon." He'd like to see what they'd make of that!

"I was there in his home for only fifteen minutes or so. I couldn't stay any longer than that: it was my first experience of sneaking into a house, and I was scared that someone would turn up while I was there. I checked the street to make sure that the coast was clear, slipped out the door, locked it, and replaced the key under the mat. Then I went to school. Carrying his precious pencil."

Scheherazade fell silent. From the look of it, she had gone back in time and was picturing the various things that had happened in order, one by one.

"That week was the happiest of my life," she said after a long pause. "I scribbled random things in my notebook with his pencil. I sniffed it, kissed it, rubbed my cheek with it, rolled it between my fingers. Sometimes I even stuck it in my mouth and sucked on it. Of course, it pained me that the more I wrote the shorter it got, but I couldn't help myself. If it got too short, I thought, I could always go back and get another. There were a whole bunch of used pencils in the pencil holder on his desk. He wouldn't have a clue that one was missing. And he probably still hadn't found the tampon tucked away in his drawer. That idea excited me no end—it gave me a strange ticklish sensation down below. The only way I could quell it was by grinding my knees together under my desk. It didn't bother me anymore that in the real world he never looked at me or showed that he was even aware of my existence. Because I secretly possessed something of his—a part of him, as it were."

"Sounds like sorcery," Habara said.

"You're right, it was a kind of sorcery. That hit me later, when I happened to read a book on the subject. But I was just a high school student then, so I didn't think about things that deeply. I just let my desire sweep me along. I knew if I kept breaking into his house it would prove fatal in the end. If I got caught in the act, odds were I'd get kicked out of school, and if word spread it would become difficult to go on living in this town. I told myself that over and over again. But it didn't make any difference. My mind wasn't working properly."

Ten days later, Scheherazade skipped school again and paid a second visit to the boy's house. It was eleven o'clock in the morning. As before, she fished the key from under the mat and opened the door. Again, his room was in flawless order, the bed perfectly made. First, she selected a pencil with a lot of use left in it and carefully placed it in her pencil case. Then she gingerly lay down on his bed, her hands clasped on her chest, and looked up at the ceiling. This was the bed where he slept every night. The thought made her heart beat faster—she found it difficult to breathe normally. Her lungs weren't filling with air and her throat was as dry as a bone, making each breath painful.

Scheherazade got off the bed, straightened the covers, and sat down on the floor, as she had on her first visit. She looked back up at the ceiling. I'm not quite ready for his bed, she told herself. That's still too much to handle.

This time, Scheherazade spent half an hour in the room. She pulled his notebooks from the drawer and glanced through them. She found a book report and read it. It was on *Kokoro*, a novel by Soseki Natsume, that summer's reading assignment. His handwriting was beautiful, as one would expect from a straight-A student, not an error or an omission anywhere. The grade on it was Excellent. What else could it be? Any teacher confronted with penmanship that perfect would automatically give it an Excellent, whether he bothered to read a single line or not.

Scheherazade moved on to the chest of drawers, examining its contents in order. His underwear and socks. Shirts and pants. His soccer uniform. They were all neatly folded. Nothing stained or frayed.

Everything clean and in perfect shape. Had he done the folding? Or, more likely, had his mother done it for him? Probably his mother. She felt a pang of jealousy toward the mother who could do these things for him each and every day.

Scheherazade leaned over and sniffed the clothes in the drawers. They all smelled freshly laundered and redolent of the sun. She took out a plain gray T-shirt, unfolded it, and pressed it to her face. Might not a whiff of his sweat remain under the arms? But there was nothing. Nevertheless, she held it there for some time, inhaling through her nose. She wanted to keep the shirt for herself. But that would be too risky. His clothes were so meticulously arranged and maintained. He (or his mother) probably knew the exact number of T-shirts in the drawer. If one went missing, all hell might break loose.

Abandoning that idea, Scheherazade carefully refolded the T-shirt and returned it to its proper place. The process required extreme care. Unnecessary risk had to be avoided. In its stead, she took a small badge, shaped like a soccer ball, that she found in one of the desk drawers to go along with the pencil. It seemed to date back to a team from his grade school years. It was old and likely of no particular importance. She doubted that he would miss it. At the very least, it would be some time before he noticed that it was gone. While she was at it, she checked the bottom drawer of the desk for the tampon. It was still there.

Scheherazade tried to imagine what would happen if his mother discovered the tampon. What would she think? Would she demand that he explain what on earth a tampon was doing in his desk? Or would she keep her discovery a secret, turning her dark suspicions over and over in her mind? What would a mother like that do under the circumstances? Scheherazade had no idea. But she decided to leave the tampon where it was. After all, it was her very first token.

To commemorate her second visit, Scheherazade left behind three strands of her hair. The night before, she had plucked them out, wrapped them in plastic, and sealed them in a tiny envelope. Now she took this envelope from her knapsack and slipped it into one of the old math notebooks in his drawer. The three hairs were straight and black, neither too long nor too short. No one would know whose they were without a DNA test, though they were clearly a girl's.

She left his house and went straight to school, arriving in time for her first afternoon class. Once again, she was happy and content for about ten days. She felt that he had become that much more hers. But, as you might expect, this chain of events would not end without incident. For, as Scheherazade had said, sneaking into other people's homes is highly addictive.

At this point in the story Scheherazade glanced at the bedside clock and saw that it was 4:32 p.m. "Got to get going," she said, as if to herself. She hopped out of bed and put on her plain, practical white panties, hooked her bra, slipped into her jeans, and pulled her dark blue Nike sweatshirt over her head. Then she scrubbed her hands in the bathroom, ran a brush through her hair, and drove away in her blue Mazda.

Left alone with nothing in particular to do, Habara lay in bed and ruminated on the story she had just told him, savoring it bit by bit, like a cow chewing its cud. Where was it headed? he wondered. As with all her stories, he hadn't a clue. He found it difficult to picture Scheherazade as a high school student. Was she slender then, free of the flab she carried today? School uniform, white socks, her hair in braids?

He wasn't hungry yet, so he put off preparing his dinner and went back to the book he had been reading, only to find that he couldn't concentrate. The image of Scheherazade sneaking into her classmate's room and burying her face in his shirt was too fresh in his mind. He was impatient to hear what had happened next.

Scheherazade's next visit to the House was three days later, after the weekend had passed. As always, she came bearing large paper bags stuffed with provisions. She went through the food in the fridge, replacing everything that was past its expiration date, examined the canned and bottled goods in the cupboard, checked the supply of condiments and spices to see what was running low, and wrote up a shopping list. She put some bottles of Perrier in the fridge to chill. Finally, she stacked the new books and DVDs she had brought with her on the table.

"Is there something more you need or want?"

"Can't think of anything," Habara replied.

Then, as always, the two went to bed and had sex. After an appropriate amount of foreplay, he slipped on his condom (she insisted that he use one), entered her, and, after an appropriate amount of time, ejaculated. Their sex was not exactly obligatory, but neither could it be said that their hearts were entirely in it. Basically, she seemed intent on keeping them from growing too enthusiastic. Just as a driving instructor would not want his students to show too much enthusiasm about their driving.

After casting a professional eye on the contents of his condom, Scheherazade began the latest installment of her story.

· · ·

As before, she felt happy and fulfilled for ten days after her second break-in. She tucked the soccer badge away in her pencil case and from time to time fingered it during class. She nibbled on the pencil she had taken and licked the lead. All the time she was thinking of his room. She thought of his desk, the bed where he slept, the chest of drawers packed with his clothes, his pristine white boxer shorts, and the tampon and three strands of hair she had hidden in his drawer.

Once her break-ins began she lost all interest in schoolwork. Her heart was no longer in it. In class, she either fiddled with the badge and the pencil or gave in to daydreams. When she went home, she was in no state of mind to tackle her homework. Scheherazade's grades had never been a problem. She wasn't a top student, but she was a serious girl who always did her assignments. So when her teacher called on her in class and she was unable to give a proper answer, he was more puzzled than angry. Eventually, he summoned her to the staff room during the lunch break. "What's the problem?" he asked her. "Is anything bothering you?" She could only mumble something vague about not feeling very well. After all, she could hardly come right out and say, Well, to tell the truth, there's this boy I like, and recently I've been breaking into his house in the middle of the day to steal his stuff, a pencil and a badge so far, which I secretly fiddle with during class and space out, and that guy's all I can think of these days. No, her secret was too weighty and dark to reveal to anyone—she had to bear it alone.

· · ·

"I had to keep breaking into his house," Scheherazade said. "I was compelled to. As you can imagine, it was a very risky business. I couldn't walk that tightrope indefinitely. Even I could see that. Sooner or later, someone would find me there, and the police would be called. The idea scared me to death. But, once the ball was rolling, there was no way I could stop it. Ten days after my second 'visit,' I went there again, as if my feet were moving on their own. I had no choice. I felt that if I didn't I would go off the deep end. Looking back, I think I really was a little crazy."

"Didn't it cause problems for you at school, skipping class so often?" Habara asked.

"My parents had their own business, so they were too busy to pay much attention to me. I'd never caused any problems up to then, never challenged their authority. So they figured a hands-off approach was best. Forging notes for school was a piece of cake. I knew how to copy my mother's handwriting, so I would write a simple note explaining why I had to be absent, sign it, and affix her seal. I had explained to my homeroom teacher that I had a medical problem that required me to spend half a day at the hospital from time to time. Since the teachers were racking their brains over what to do about the kids who hadn't come to school in ages, they weren't too concerned about me taking half a day off every now and then."

Scheherazade shot a quick glance at the clock next to the bed before continuing.

"I got the key from under the mat and entered the house for a third time. It was as quiet as before—no, even quieter, for some reason. It rattled me when the refrigerator turned on—it sounded like a huge beast sighing.

The phone rang while I was there. The ringing was so loud and harsh that I thought my heart would stop. I was covered with sweat. No one picked up, of course, and it stopped after about ten rings. The house felt even quieter then."

Scheherazade spent a long time stretched out on his bed that day. This time her heart did not pound so wildly, and she was able to breathe normally. She could imagine him sleeping peacefully beside her, even feel as if she were watching over him as he slept. She felt that, if she reached out, she could touch his muscular arm. He wasn't there next to her, of course. She was just lost in a haze of daydreams.

She felt an overpowering urge to smell him. Rising from the bed, she walked over to his chest of drawers, opened one, and examined the shirts inside. All had been thoroughly washed and dried in the sun, then neatly folded and rolled like cake. They were pristine, and free of odor, just like before.

Then an idea struck her. It just might work. She raced down the stairs to the first floor. There, in the room beside the bath, she found the laundry hamper and removed the lid. Mixed together were the soiled clothes of the three family members—mother, daughter, and son. A day's worth, from the looks of it. Scheherazade extracted a single piece of male clothing. A white crewneck T-shirt. She took a whiff. The unmistakable scent of a young man. A mustiness she had smelled before, when her male classmates were close by. Not a scintillating odor, to be sure. But the fact that this smell was *his* brought Scheherazade unbounded joy. When she put her nose next to the armpits and inhaled, she felt as though she were in his embrace, his arms wrapped firmly about her.

T-shirt in hand, Scheherazade climbed the stairs to the second floor and lay on his bed once more. She buried her face in his shirt and greedily breathed in the sweaty fragrance. Now she could feel a languid sensation in the lower part of her body. Her nipples were stiffening as well. Could her period be on the way? No, it was much too early. Was this sexual desire? If so, then what could she do about it? Was there a way? She had no idea. One thing was certain, though—there was nothing to be done under these circumstances. Not here in his room, on his bed.

In the end, Scheherazade decided to take the sweaty shirt home with her. It was risky, for sure. His mother was likely to figure out that a shirt was missing. Even if she didn't realize it had been stolen, she would still shake her head and wonder where it had gone. Any woman who kept her house so spotless was bound to be a neat freak of the first order. When something went missing, she would search the house from top to bottom until she found it. Like a keen-nosed police dog. Undoubtedly, she would uncover the traces of Scheherazade in her precious son's room. But, even as Scheherazade understood this, she didn't want to part with the shirt. Her brain was powerless to persuade her heart.

Instead, she began thinking about what to leave behind. Her panties seemed like the best choice. They were of an ordinary sort, simple, relatively new, and fresh that morning. She could hide them at the very back of his closet. Could there be anything more appropriate to leave in exchange? But, when she took them off, the crotch was damp. I guess this comes from desire, too, she thought. She sniffed them but there was no odor. Still, it would hardly do to leave something tainted by her lust in his room. She would only be degrading herself. She slipped them back on and began to think about what else to leave. What should it be?

Scheherazade broke off her story. For a long time, she didn't say a word. She lay there breathing quietly with her eyes closed. Beside her, Habara followed suit, waiting for her to resume.

At last, she opened her eyes and spoke. "Hey, Mr. Habara," she said. It was the first time she had addressed him by name.

Habara looked at her.

"Do you think we could do it one more time?"

"I think I could manage that," he said.

So they made love again. This time, though, her body was very different from before. When he entered her she was soft and wet. Her skin was taut too, and it glowed. Habara guessed that she was reliving her days of breaking and entering. That memory must be very vivid. Or perhaps it wasn't a memory at all; perhaps she had *actually* gone back in time to her seventeen-year-old self. In the same way she revisited her former lives. Scheherazade was capable of that sort of thing. She was able to direct her incredible storytelling powers at herself. Like a master hypnotist hypnotizing himself by looking in a mirror.

The two of them made love as never before. Violently, passionately, and at length. Her climax at the end was unmistakable. A series of powerful spasms that left her trembling. She looked entirely different at that moment: even her face was transformed. For Habara, it was like peering through a crack to catch a brief glimpse of Scheherazade in her youth—now he had a good idea of what she had looked like then: the woman in his arms was a troubled seventeen-year-old girl who had somehow become trapped in the body of a thirty-five-year-old housewife. Habara was sure of it. He could feel her in there, her eyes closed, her body quivering, innocently inhaling the aroma of a boy's sweaty T-shirt.

This time, Scheherazade did not tell him a story after sex. Nor did she check the contents of his condom. They lay there quietly next to each other. Her eyes were wide open, and she was staring at the ceiling. Like a lamprey gazing up at the bright surface of the water. How wonderful it would be, Habara thought, if he, too, could inhabit another time or space—leave this single, clearly defined human being named Nobutaka Habara behind and become a nameless lamprey. He pictured himself and Scheherazade side by side, their suckers fastened to a rock, their bodies waving in the current, eying the surface as they waited for a fat trout to swim smugly by.

"So what did you leave in exchange for the shirt?" Habara broke the silence.

She did not reply immediately.

"Nothing," she said at last. "Nothing I had brought along could come close to that shirt with his odor. So I just took it and sneaked out. That was when I became a burglar, pure and simple."

．　．　．

When, twelve days later, Scheherazade went back to the boy's house for the fourth time, there was a new lock on the front door. Its gold color gleamed in the midday sun, as if to boast of its great sturdiness. And there was no key hidden under the mat. Clearly, his mother's suspicions had been aroused by the missing shirt. She must have searched high and low, coming across other signs that told of something strange going on in her house. Just possibly, someone had entered in her family's absence. Quickly, she had the lock replaced. Her instincts had been unerring, her reaction swift.

Scheherazade was, of course, disappointed by this development, but at the same time she felt relieved. It was as if someone had stepped behind her and removed a great weight from her shoulders. This means I don't have to go on breaking into his house, she thought. There was no doubt that, had the lock not been changed, her invasions would have gone on indefinitely. Nor was there any doubt that her actions would have escalated with each visit. It was a road leading to a catastrophe of some sort. Eventually, a member of the family would have shown up while she was on the second floor. There would have been no avenue of escape. No way to talk herself out of her predicament. This was the future that had been awaiting her, sooner or later, and the outcome would have been devastating. Now she had dodged it. Perhaps she should thank his mother—though she had never met the woman—for having eyes like a hawk.

Scheherazade inhaled the aroma of his T-shirt each night before she went to bed. She slept with it next to her. She would wrap it in paper and hide it before she left for school in the morning. Then, after dinner, she would pull it out to caress and sniff. She worried that the odor might fade as the days went by, but that didn't happen. Like an undying memory of singular importance, the smell of his sweat had permeated his shirt for good.

Now that further break-ins were out of the question—which was okay with her—Scheherazade's state of mind slowly began to return to normal. She daydreamed less in class, and her teacher's words began to register. Nevertheless, her chief focus was not on her teacher's voice but on her classmate's behavior. She kept her eye discreetly trained on him, trying to detect a change, any indication at all that he might be nervous about something. But he acted exactly the same as always. He threw his head back and laughed as unaffectedly as ever, and answered promptly when called upon. He shouted as loudly in soccer practice and got just as sweaty. She could see no trace of anything out of the ordinary—just an upright young man, leading a seemingly unclouded existence.

Still, Scheherazade knew of one shadow that was hanging over him. Or something close to that. No one else knew, in all likelihood. Just her (and, come to think of it, possibly his mother). On her third break-in, she had come across a number of pornographic magazines cleverly concealed in the farthest recesses of his closet. They were full of pictures of naked women, spreading their legs and offering generous views of their genitals. Some pictures portrayed the act of sex: men inserted rodlike penises into female bodies in the most unnatural of positions. Scheherazade had never laid eyes on photographs like these before. She sat at his desk and flipped slowly through the magazines, studying each photo with great interest. She guessed that he masturbated while viewing them. But the idea did not strike her as especially repulsive. Nor did she feel at all let down having seen this side of him. She accepted masturbation as a perfectly normal activity. All those sperm had to go somewhere, just as girls had to have periods. In other words, he was a typical teenager. Neither hero nor saint. She found that knowledge something of a relief.

"When my break-ins stopped, my passion for him began to cool. It was gradual, like the tide ebbing from a long, sloping beach. Somehow or other, I found myself smelling his shirt less often and spending less time caressing his pencil and badge. The fever was passing. What I had contracted was not something *like* sickness but the real thing. As long as it lasted, I couldn't think straight. Maybe everybody goes through a crazy period like that at one time or another. Or maybe it was something that happened only to me. How about you? Did you ever have an experience like that?"

Habara tried to remember, but drew a blank. "No, nothing that extreme, I don't think," he said.

Scheherazade looked somewhat disappointed by his answer.

"Anyway, I forgot all about him once I graduated. So quickly and easily, it was weird. What was it about him that had made the seventeen-year-old me fall so hard? Try as I might, I couldn't remember. Life is strange, isn't it? You can be totally entranced by the glow of something one minute, be willing to sacrifice everything to make it yours, but then a little time passes, or your perspective changes a bit, and all of a sudden you're shocked at how faded it appears. What was I looking at? you wonder. So that's the story of my 'breaking-and-entering' period."

She made it sound like Picasso's Blue Period, Habara thought. But he had a good idea what she was trying to explain.

She glanced at the digital clock next to the bed. The time for her to leave was drawing near. There was a pregnant pause.

"To tell the truth," she said finally, "the story doesn't end there. A few years later, when I was in my second year of nursing school, a strange stroke of fate brought us together again. His mother played a big role in it; in fact, there was something spooky about the whole thing—it was like one of those old ghost stories. Events took a rather unbelievable course. Would you like to hear about it?"

"I'd love to," Habara said.

"It had better wait till my next visit," Scheherazade said. "Once I get started it'll take time, and it's getting late. I've got to head home and fix dinner."

She got out of bed and put on her clothes—panties, stockings, camisole, and, finally, her skirt and blouse. Habara casually watched the sequence of her movements from the bed. It struck him that the way women put on their clothes could be even more interesting than the way they took them off.

"Any books in particular you'd like me to pick up?" she asked, on her way out the door.

No, not especially, he answered. What he really wanted, he thought, was for her to tell him the rest of her story, but he didn't put that into words. Doing so might jeopardize his chances of ever hearing it.

Habara went to bed early that night and thought about Scheherazade. Perhaps he would never see her again. That worried him. The possibility was just too real. Nothing of a personal nature—no vow, no implicit understanding— held them together. Theirs was a chance relationship created by someone else, and might be terminated on that person's whim. In other words, they were attached, and barely at that, by a slender thread. It was likely—no, certain—that that thread would eventually be broken. The only question was whether that would occur sooner or later. Once Scheherazade was gone, he would no longer be able to hear her stories. When their flow was broken, all the strange and unknown tales she should have told him would vanish without ever being heard.

But there was another possibility. He could be deprived of his freedom entirely, in which case not only Scheherazade but all women might be taken away from him. It was a very real prospect. Never again would he be able to enter the warm moistness of their bodies. Never again would he feel them quiver in response. Perhaps an even more distressing prospect for Habara than the cessation of sexual activity, however, was the loss of the moments of shared intimacy. To lose all contact with women was, in the end, to lose that connection. What his time spent with women offered was the opportunity to be embraced by reality, on the one hand, while negating it entirely on the other. That was something Scheherazade had provided in abundance—indeed, her gift was inexhaustible. The prospect of losing that made him saddest of all.

Habara closed his eyes and stopped thinking of Scheherazade. Instead, he thought of lampreys. Of jawless lampreys fastened to rocks, hiding among the waterweeds, swaying back and forth in the current. He imagined that he was one of them, waiting for a trout to appear. But no trout passed by, no matter how long he waited. Not a fat one, not a skinny one, no trout at all. Eventually the sun went down, and his surroundings were enfolded in deep darkness.

Translated by Ted Goossen

KINO

THE MAN ALWAYS SAT IN THE SAME SEAT, the stool farthest down the counter. When it wasn't occupied, that is,
though it was nearly always empty. The bar was seldom
crowded, and that particular seat was the most incon-
spicuous and the least comfortable. A staircase in the
back made the ceiling slanted and low, so it was hard to
stand up there without bumping your head. The man
was tall, yet, for some reason, he preferred that cramped,
narrow spot.

Kino remembered the first time the man had come
to his bar. His appearance had immediately caught
Kino's eye—the bluish shaved head, the thin build yet
broad shoulders, the keen glint in his eye, the prominent
cheekbones and wide forehead. He looked to be in his
early thirties, and he wore a long gray raincoat, though
it wasn't raining and didn't seem about to rain anytime
soon. At first, Kino tagged him as a yakuza, and was on
his guard around him. It was seven thirty on a chilly
mid-April evening, and the bar was empty.

The man chose the seat at the end of the counter, took off his coat, hung it on a hook on the wall, in a quiet voice ordered a beer, then silently read a thick book. From his expression he seemed totally absorbed in what he was reading. After half an hour, finished with the beer, he raised his hand an inch or two to motion Kino over, and ordered a whiskey. "Which brand?" Kino asked, but the man said he had no preference.

"Just an ordinary sort of Scotch. A double. Add an equal amount of water and a little bit of ice, if you would."

An ordinary sort of Scotch? Kino poured some White Label into a glass, added the same amount of water, chipped off ice with an ice pick, and added two small, nicely formed ice cubes. The man took a sip, scrutinized the glass, and narrowed his eyes. "This will do fine."

He read for another half hour, then stood up and paid his bill in cash. He counted out exact change so that he wouldn't get any coins back. Kino breathed a small sigh of relief as soon as he was out the door. But after the man had left his presence remained. As Kino stood behind the counter, preparing some dishes, he glanced up occasionally at the seat the man had occupied. It felt like someone was still there, raising his hand a couple of inches to order something.

The man began coming regularly to Kino's bar. Once, at most twice, a week. He would invariably have a beer first, then a whiskey. (White Label, equal amount of water, plus a few ice cubes.) Sometimes he had two glasses of whiskey, though usually restricted himself to one. Occasionally he would study the day's menu on the blackboard and order a light meal.

The man hardly ever said a word. Even after he started

frequenting the bar, he never spoke other than to order something. He gave Kino a small nod each time he saw him, as if to tell him he remembered his face. He always came fairly early in the evening, a book, tucked under his arm, that he would place on the counter. Always a thick hardbound book. Kino never saw him read a paperback. Whenever he got tired of reading (at least, Kino guessed that he was tired), he looked up from the page and studied the bottles of liquor lined up on the shelves in front of him, as if examining a series of unusual taxidermied animals from faraway lands.

Once Kino got used to the man, though, he never felt uncomfortable around him, even when it was just the two of them. Kino never spoke much himself, and didn't find it hard to remain silent around others. While the man read, Kino did what he would do if he were alone— wash dishes, prepare sauces, choose records to play, or page through the newspaper.

Kino didn't know the man's name, though the man knew he was Kino, since that was the name of the bar. But the man never introduced himself and Kino never bothered to ask. The man was just a regular customer who came to the bar, enjoyed a beer and a whiskey, read silently, paid in cash, then left. He never bothered anybody else. What more did Kino need to know about him?

Kino had worked for a sports equipment maker for seventeen years. Back in college, he had been a standout middle-distance runner, but in his junior year he'd torn his Achilles tendon and had to give up on the idea of joining a corporate track team. After graduation, on his coach's recommendation, he got a job at the sports equipment company. At work, he was in charge of persuading sports stores to stock his brand of running shoes and leading athletes to try them out. The company, a mid-level firm headquartered in Okayama, was far from well known, certainly no Mizuno or Asics, and it lacked the financial power of a Nike or an Adidas to draw up exclusive contracts with the world's best runners. They couldn't even pay to entertain famous athletes, and if Kino wanted to take a runner to dinner he either had to reduce his own travel expenses or pay out of his own pocket.

Still, his company made carefully handcrafted shoes for top athletes, with little regard for the bottom line, and that craftsman-like care eventually paid off, with quite a few athletes who swore by their products. "Do an honest job and it will pay off" was the slogan of the company's founder, and that low-key, somewhat anachronistic corporate approach suited Kino's personality. Even a taciturn, unsociable man like him was able to make a go of sales. Actually, it was because of his personality that coaches trusted him and athletes (though not all that many in total) took a liking to him. He listened carefully to each runner's needs, what specifications they wanted in a shoe, and made sure the head of manufacturing got all the details. He found the job engaging, and satisfying. The pay wasn't much to speak of, but the job suited him. Although he couldn't run anymore himself, he loved seeing the runners race around the track, their form textbook perfect.

When Kino quit his job, it wasn't because he was dissatisfied with his work but because he discovered that his wife was having an affair with his best friend at the company. Kino spent more time out on the road than at home in Tokyo. He'd stuff a large gym bag full of shoe samples and make the rounds of sporting goods stores all over Japan, also visiting local colleges and companies that sponsored track teams. His wife and his colleague started sleeping together while he was away. Kino wasn't the type who easily picked up on clues. He thought everything was fine with his marriage, and nothing his wife said or did tipped him off to the contrary. If he hadn't happened to come home from a business trip a day early, he might never have discovered what was going on.

When he got back to Tokyo that day, he went straight to his condo in Kasai, only to find his wife and his friend naked and entwined in his bedroom, in the bed where he and his wife slept. It was obvious what they were up to. His wife was on top, crouched over the man, and when Kino opened the door he came face-to-face with her and her lovely breasts bouncing up and down. He was thirty-nine then, his wife thirty-five. They had no children. Kino lowered his head, shut the bedroom door, left the apartment, lugging his shoulder bag stuffed with a week's worth of laundry, and never went back. The next day, he quit his job.

Kino had an unmarried aunt, his mother's attractive, older sister. Ever since he was a child, his aunt had been nice to him. She'd had an older boyfriend for many years ("lover" might be the more accurate term), and he had generously given her a small house in Aoyama. Back in the good old days. She lived on the second floor of the house, and ran a coffee shop on the first floor. In front was a small garden and an impressive willow tree, with low-hanging, leafy branches. The house was on a narrow backstreet behind the Nezu Museum, not exactly the best location for drawing customers, but his aunt had a gift for attracting people, and her coffee shop did a decent amount of business.

After she turned sixty, though, she hurt her back, and it became increasingly difficult for her to run the shop alone. She decided to close the business and move to the Izu Kogen Highlands, to a resort condo with attached hot springs and a rehabilitation center. "I was wondering if eventually you might want to take over the shop?" she asked Kino. This was three months before he discovered his wife's affair. "I appreciate the offer," he told her, "but right now I don't feel like doing that."

After he submitted his resignation at work, he phoned his aunt to ask if she'd sold the shop yet. It was listed with a real estate agent, she told him, but no serious offers had come in. "I'd like to open a bar there if I can," Kino said. "Could I pay you rent by the month?"

"But what about your job?" she asked.

"I quit a couple of days ago."

"Didn't your wife have a problem with that?"

"We're probably going to get divorced soon."

Kino didn't explain the reason, and his aunt didn't ask. There was silence for a time on the other end of the line. Then his aunt named a figure for the monthly rent, far lower than what Kino had expected. "I think I can handle that," he told her.

"I'll be getting some severance pay," he went on, "so I won't make any trouble for you when it comes to paying."

"That doesn't worry me at all," his aunt said decisively.

He and his aunt had never talked all that much (his

mother had discouraged him from getting close to her), but they'd always seemed to have, strangely enough, a kind of mutual understanding. She knew that Kino wasn't the type of person to break a promise.

Kino used half of his savings to transform the coffee shop into a bar. He purchased the simplest furniture he could find, and had a long, sturdy bar installed, and bought all-new chairs. He put up new wallpaper in a calming color, and installed lighting more in keeping with a place where people went to drink. He brought his meager record collection from home, and lined a shelf in the bar with LPs. He owned a fairly decent stereo—a Thorens turntable, a Luxman amp, and small JBL two-way speakers—that he'd bought when he was single, a fairly extravagant purchase back then. But he had always enjoyed listening to old jazz records. It was his only hobby, one that he didn't share with anyone else he knew. In college, he'd worked part time as a bartender at a pub in Roppongi, so he was well versed in the art of mixing cocktails.

He called his bar Kino. He couldn't come up with a better name. The first week he was open, he didn't have a single customer. He had anticipated this, though, and wasn't perturbed. After all, he hadn't told anyone he knew that he was opening a bar. He hadn't advertised the place, or even put out an eye-catching sign. He simply waited patiently for curious people to stumble across this little backstreet bar. He still had some of his severance pay, and his wife hadn't asked for any financial support. She was already living with his former colleague, and they no longer needed the condo in Kasai, so they decided to sell it. After paying back what they owed on the mortgage, they split the remaining sum. Kino lived on the second floor of his aunt's house, and it looked as though, for the time being, he'd be able to get by.

As he waited for his first customer, Kino enjoyed listening to whatever music he liked and reading books he'd been wanting to read. Like dry ground welcoming the rain, he let the solitude, silence, and loneliness soak in. He listened to a lot of Art Tatum solo piano pieces. Somehow they seemed to fit his mood.

He wasn't sure why, but he felt no anger or bitterness toward his wife, or the colleague she was sleeping with. The betrayal had been a shock, for sure, but, as time passed, he began to feel as if it couldn't have been helped, as if this had been his fate all along. In his life, after all, he had achieved nothing, had been totally unproductive. He couldn't make anyone else happy, and, of course, couldn't make himself happy. Happiness? He wasn't even sure what that meant. He didn't have a clear sense, either, of emotions like pain or anger, disappointment or resignation, and how they were supposed to feel. The most he could do was create a place where his heart—devoid now of any depth or weight—could be tethered, to keep it from wandering aimlessly. This little bar, Kino, tucked into a backstreet, became that place. And it became, too—not by design, exactly—a strangely comfortable space.

It wasn't a person who first discovered what a comfortable place Kino was but a stray cat. A young gray female with a long, lovely tail. The cat favored a sunken display case in a corner of the bar and liked to curl up there to sleep. Kino didn't pay much attention to the cat, figuring it wanted to be left alone. Once a day, he fed it and changed its water, but nothing beyond that. And he constructed a small pet door so that it could go in and out of the bar whenever it liked. The cat, though, preferred entering and exiting the bar along with people, through the front door.

The cat may have brought some good luck along with it, for after it appeared so did a scattering of customers. Some of them started to come by regularly—ones who took a liking to this little backstreet bar with its small sign, wonderful old willow tree, its quiet middle-aged owner, vintage records spinning on a turntable, limited menu of two new dishes per day, gray cat sacked out in a corner. And these people sometimes brought other new customers. Still far from thriving, the bar at least earned back the rent. For Kino, that was enough.

The young man with the shaved head started coming to the bar about two months after it opened. And it was another two months before Kino learned his name. My name is Kamita, he said. It's written with the characters for "god"—*kami*—and "field"—"god's field," the man explained, but isn't pronounced "Kanda," as you might expect. It's pronounced "Kamita." He wasn't addressing Kino when he said this, though.

It was raining lightly that day, the kind of rain where you aren't sure if you really need an umbrella. There were just three customers in the bar, Kamita and two men in dark suits. It was seven thirty. As always, Kamita was at the farthest stool down the counter, sipping a White Label and water and reading. The two men were seated at a table, drinking a bottle of Haut-Médoc. They had brought the bottle with them in a paper bag, and asked Kino if he would mind their drinking it there, for a five-thousand-yen cork fee. It was a first for Kino, but he had no reason to refuse. He opened the bottle and set down two wineglasses and a bowl of mixed nuts. Not much trouble at all. The two men smoked a lot, though, which for Kino, who hated cigarette smoke, made them less welcome. With little else to do, Kino sat on a stool and listened to the Coleman Hawkins LP with the track "Joshua Fit the Battle of Jericho." He found the bass solo by Major Holley amazing.

At first, the two men seemed to be getting along fine, enjoying their wine, but then a difference of opinion arose on some topic or other—what it was, Kino had no idea—and the men grew steadily more worked up, and what had begun as a minor disagreement escalated to a full-blown argument. At some point, one of them stood, tipping the table and sending the full ashtray and one of the wineglasses crashing to the floor. Kino hurried over with a broom, swept up the mess, and put a clean glass and ashtray on the table.

Kamita—though at this time Kino had yet to learn his name—was clearly disgusted by the men's behavior. His expression didn't change, but he kept tapping the fingers of his left hand lightly on the counter, like a pianist checking one particular key. I have to get this situation under control, Kino realized, I need to step forward and take care of this. He went over to the men. "I'm sorry," he said politely, "but I wonder if you'd mind keeping your voices down a bit."

One of them looked up at him with a cold glint in his eye and rose from the table. Kino hadn't noticed it until now, but the man was huge. He wasn't so much tall as barrel-chested, with enormous arms, the sort of build you'd expect of a sumo wrestler. The type of person who had never once, since childhood, lost a fight; the sort of person who was used to bossing others around and couldn't stand to be told what to do. Kino had met a few people like this back in college. You simply couldn't reason with them.

The other man was much smaller. Thin and pale, with a shrewd look, the type who was good at egging people on. He slowly got up from his seat, too, and Kino found himself face-to-face with both of them. The men had apparently decided to use this opportunity to call a halt to their quarrel and jointly confront Kino. They were perfectly coordinated, almost as if they had secretly been waiting for this very situation to arise.

"So, you think you can just butt in and interrupt us?" the larger of the two said, his voice hard and low.

The suits they wore seemed expensive, but closer inspection showed them to be tacky and poorly made. Not full-fledged yakuza, though whatever work they were involved in was, clearly, not respectable. The larger man had a crew cut, while his companion's hair was dyed brown and pulled back in a high ponytail. Kino steeled himself for something bad to happen. Sweat began to pour from his armpits.

"Pardon me," another voice said.

Kino turned to find that Kamita was standing behind him.

"Don't blame the staff," Kamita said, pointing to Kino. "I'm the one who asked him to request that you keep it down. It makes it hard to concentrate, and I can't read my book."

Kamita's voice was calmer, more languid, than usual. But something, unseen, was beginning to stir.

"'Can't read my book,'" the smaller man repeated in low voice, as if making sure that there was nothing ungrammatical about the sentence.

"What, don't ya got a home?" the larger man asked Kamita.

"I do," Kamita replied. "I live nearby."

"Then why don't ya go home and read there?"

"I like reading here," Kamita said.

The two men exchanged a look.

"Hand over the book," the smaller man said. "I'll read it for you."

"I like to read by myself, quietly," Kamita said. "And I'd hate it if you mispronounced any of the words."

"Aren't you a piece of work," the larger man said. "What a funny guy."

"What's your name, anyway?" Ponytail asked.

"My name is Kamita," he said. "It's written with the characters for 'god'—*kami*—and 'field': 'god's field.' But it isn't pronounced 'Kanda,' as you might expect. It's pronounced 'Kamita.'" Thus Kino first learned his name.

"I'll remember that," the large man said.

"Good idea. Memories can be useful," Kamita said.

"Anyway, how about we step outside?" the smaller man said. "That way, we can say exactly what we want to."

"Fine with me," Kamita said. "Anywhere you say. But, before we do that, could you pay your check? You don't want to cause the bar any trouble."

"All right," the smaller one agreed.

Kamita asked Kino to bring over their check, and he laid exact change for his own drink on the counter.

Ponytail extracted a ten-thousand-yen bill from his wallet and tossed it onto the table.

"Will that cover it, including the broken glass?"

"That's plenty," Kino said.

"What a cheap joint," the large man said, sneeringly.

"I don't need any change back," Ponytail told Kino. "But why don't ya buy yourself some better wineglasses? This is expensive wine, and glasses like these make it taste like shit."

"What a cheap joint," the larger man said again, sneeringly.

"Correct. A cheap bar with cheap customers," Kamita said. "It doesn't suit you. There's got to be somewhere else that does. Not that I know where."

"Now, aren't you the wise guy," the large man said. "You make me laugh."

"Think it over later on, and have a good, long laugh," Kamita said.

"No way you're gonna tell me where I should go," Ponytail said. He slowly licked his lips, like a snake sizing up its prey.

The large man opened the door and stepped outside, Ponytail following behind. Perhaps sensing the tension in the air, the cat, despite the rain, leaped outside after them.

"Are you sure you're okay?" Kino asked Kamita.

"Not to worry," Kamita said, with a slight smile. "You don't need to do anything, Mr. Kino. Just stay put. This will be over soon."

Kamita went outside and shut the door. It was still raining, a little harder than before. Kino sat down on a stool and waited. There was no sign of any new customers. It was oddly still outside, and he couldn't hear a thing. Kamita's book lay open on the counter, like a well-trained dog waiting for its master. About ten minutes later, the door opened, and in strode Kamita, alone.

"Would you mind lending me a towel?" he asked.

Kino handed him a fresh towel, and Kamita wiped his head. Then his neck, face, and, finally, both hands. "Thank you. Everything's okay now," he said. "Those two won't be showing their faces here again. They won't bother you anymore."

"What in the world happened?"

Kamita just shook his head, as if to say, "Better you don't know." He went over to his seat, downed the rest of his whiskey, and picked up where he'd left off in his book.

Later, as he was leaving, he went to pay the check, but Kino reminded him he had already paid. "Ah, right you are," Kamita said, wryly, then raised the collar of his raincoat, put on his round, brimmed hat, and left.

That evening, after Kamita had gone, Kino went outside and made a circuit of the neighborhood. The alley was deserted and quiet. No signs of a fight, no trace of blood. He couldn't imagine what had taken place. He went back to the bar to wait for other customers, but no one else came that night. The cat didn't return, either. He poured himself some White Label, a double, added an equal amount of water and two small ice cubes, and tasted it. Nothing special, about what you'd expect. But that night he needed a shot of alcohol in his system.

One day when Kino was in college, he was walking the backstreets of Shinjuku when he came across a man, a yakuza by the look of him, quarreling with two young company employees. The yakuza was a shabby-looking and middle-aged man and the two company men were well built and also a little drunk, so they underestimated their opponent. The yakuza must have had some boxing skills, for at a certain point he made a fist and, without a word, knocked them down with lightning-quick blows. Once they were down he kicked them hard, over and over, with the soles of his leather shoes. Probably broke a few of their ribs. Kino could still hear the dull crack. Then the man turned and walked away, like nothing had happened. This is the way a professional fights, Kino thought at the time. No superfluous words. Everything mentally choreographed beforehand. Put the other guy on the ground before he has a chance to get ready. And once he's down, make sure he stays down for good. Then turn and walk away. No way an amateur could stand up to that.

Kino imagined Kamita doing the same, knocking the two men down in the space of a couple of seconds. Come to think of it, Kamita did sort of remind him of a boxer. But Kino had no way of knowing what actually happened on that rainy night. Kamita never explained, and the more Kino thought about it, the deeper the mystery became.

About a week after the incident, Kino slept with a female customer. She was the first woman he'd had sex with since he left his wife. She was thirty, or perhaps a little older. Somewhere in that vicinity. He wasn't sure if she would be classified as beautiful, but she had long, straight hair, a short nose, and something special about her, something that stood out. Her demeanor and way of speaking was slow and langorous, and it was hard to read anything in her expression.

The woman had been to the bar several times before, always in the company of a man of about the same age who wore tortoiseshell-framed glasses and a beatnik-like goatee. He had unruly hair and never wore a tie, so Kino figured he was probably not your typical company employee. The woman always wore a tight-fitting dress that showed off her slender, shapely figure. They sat at the bar, exchanging an occasional hushed word or two as they sipped cocktails or sherry. They never stayed long. Kino imagined they were having a drink before they made love. Or else after. He couldn't say which, but the way they drank reminded him of sex. Drawn-out, intense sex. The two of them were strangely expressionless, especially the woman, whom Kino had never seen smile.

The woman spoke to him sometimes, always about the music that was playing. The names of the musicians or the title of the track. She liked jazz too, and collected records. "My father used to listen to this music at home a lot," she told him. "I prefer more contemporary music, but hearing this kind of music brings back a lot of memories." From her tone, Kino couldn't tell if the memories were of the music or of her father. But he didn't venture to ask.

Kino actually tried not to have too much to do with the woman. It was clear that the man wasn't very pleased when he was friendly to her. One time he and the woman did have a lengthy conversation—exchanging tips on used-record stores in Tokyo and the best way to take care of vinyl—and, after that, the man kept shooting him cold, suspicious looks. Kino was usually careful to keep his distance from any sort of entanglement. Among human emotions, nothing was worse than jealousy and pride, and Kino had had a number of awful experiences because of one or the other. It struck him at times that there was something about him that stirred up the dark side in other people.

That night, though, the woman came to the bar alone. There were no other customers. It had been raining for a long time, and when she opened the door cool night air crept into the bar, carrying with it the scent of rain. She sat at the counter, ordered a brandy, and asked Kino to play some Billie Holiday. "Something really old, if you could." Kino put a Columbia record on the turntable, one with the track "Georgia on My Mind." The two of them listened silently. "Could you play the other side, too?" she asked, when it ended, and he did as she requested.

She slowly worked her way through three brandies, listening to a few more records—Erroll Garner's "Moonglow," Buddy DeFranco's "I Can't Get Started." At first, Kino thought she was waiting for the man, but by the time he was ready to close, the man still had not shown up. Apparently she wasn't waiting. She hadn't glanced at her watch even once. She wore a thin dark blue cardigan over a short-sleeve black dress, and small imitation-pearl earrings. She just sat there, listening to the music, lost in thought, sipping her brandy. The woman didn't seem to mind not talking. Brandy was a drink that went well with silence—you gently swirled it, appreciated the color, inhaled the fragrance.

"Your friend isn't coming today?" Kino decided to ask as closing time drew near.

"He isn't coming. He's far away," the woman said. She stood up from the stool and walked over to where the cat lay sleeping. She gently stroked its back with her fingertips. The cat, unperturbed, went on sleeping.

"We're thinking of not seeing each other anymore," the woman said. He wasn't sure if she was addressing him, or the cat.

Either way, Kino didn't know how to respond, so he said nothing, and continued to straighten up behind the counter. He cleaned the grill, washed the cooking utensils, and stowed them away in drawers.

"I'm not sure how to put it," the woman said. She stopped petting the cat and went back to the bar, high heels clicking. "Our relationship isn't exactly . . . normal."

"Not exactly normal." Kino repeated her words without really considering what they meant.

She finished the small amount of brandy left in her glass. "I have something I'd like to show you, Mr. Kino," she said.

Whatever it was, Kino didn't want to see it. It wasn't something that should be seen. Of that he was certain. But he had lost words to say so.

The woman removed her cardigan and placed it on the stool. She reached both hands behind her and unzipped her dress. She turned her back to Kino. Just below her white bra clasp he saw an irregular sprinkling of small marks the color of faded charcoal, like bruises. They reminded him of constellations in the winter sky. A dark row of depleted stars. It may have been the trace of a rash from a contagious disease. Or scars.

The woman said nothing, just displayed her bare back to Kino for a while. The bright white of her new bra and the darkness of the marks made for an ominous contrast. Like someone who cannot even comprehend the meaning of the question he has been asked, Kino just stared wordlessly at her back. Finally, she zipped up and turned to face him. She put on her cardigan and fixed her hair.

"Those are cigarette burns," she said simply.

Kino was at a loss for words. But he had to say something. "Who did that to you?" he asked, his voice parched.

The woman didn't reply. She didn't even seem about to, and Kino realized that he wasn't hoping for an answer.

"Could I get another brandy?" the woman asked.

Kino freshened her drink. She took a sip, feeling the warmth slowly spread down her throat.

"Mr. Kino?"

Kino stopped polishing a glass and looked up.

"I have them in other places, too," she said finally, her voice drained of expression. "Places that are . . . a little hard to show."

Kino couldn't remember now what had led him to sleep with the woman that night. Kino had felt, from the first, that there was something out of the ordinary about her. Something had triggered an instinctive response, warning him not to get involved. And now these cigarette burns on her back. He was basically a cautious person. If he really needed to sleep with a woman, he could always make do with a professional, he felt. Just take care of things by paying for it. And it wasn't as if he were even attracted to this woman.

But that night she desperately wanted a man to make love to her—and it seemed that he was the man. Her eyes were depthless, the pupils strangely dilated, but there was a decisive glitter in them that would brook no retreat. Kino didn't have the power to resist.

He locked up the bar, and the two of them went upstairs. In the light of the bedroom, the woman quickly took off her dress, peeled off her underwear, and showed him the places that were a little hard to show. Kino couldn't help averting his eyes at first, but then was drawn back to look. He couldn't understand, nor did he want to understand, the mind of a man who would do something so cruel, or of a woman who would willingly endure it. It was a savage scene from a barren planet, light-years away from where Kino lived.

The woman took his hand and guided it to the scars, making him touch each one in turn. There were scars on her breasts, and beside her vagina. She guided his hand as he traced those dark, hard marks, as if he were using a pencil to connect the dots. The marks seemed to form a shape that reminded him of something, but in the end led nowhere. They had sex on the tatami floor. No words exchanged, no foreplay, no time even to turn off the light or lay out the futon. The woman's tongue slid down his throat, her nails dug into his back. Under the light, like two starving animals, they devoured the flesh they craved, over and over. In all sorts of positions, almost without ceasing. When dawn began to show outside, they crawled onto the futon and slept, as if dragged down into darkness. Kino awoke just before noon, and the woman was gone. He felt as if he'd had a very realistic dream, but, of course, it hadn't been a dream. His back was lined with scratches, his arms with bite marks, his penis wrung by a dull ache. Several long black hairs swirled around his white pillow, and the sheets had a strong scent he'd never smelled before.

The woman came to the bar several times after that, always with the goateed man. They would sit at the counter, speak in subdued voices as they drank a cocktail or two, and then leave. The woman would exchange a few words with Kino, mostly about music. Her tone was the same as before, as if she had no memory of what had taken place between them that night. Still, Kino could detect a glint of desire in her eyes, like a faint light deep down a mineshaft. He was sure of it. It was definitely there. And it brought everything vividly back to him— the stab of her nails into his back, the sting of his penis, her long, slithering tongue, the odor on his bedding. You can't forget that, the light told him.

As he and the woman spoke, the man with her, like a careful reader adept at reading between the lines, observed Kino's expression and behavior. Kino sensed something viscous entwining itself about the couple, as if there were a deep secret only the two of them shared. As before, he couldn't tell if they came to the bar right before, or right after, they had sex. But it was definitely one or the other. And he noticed that, oddly, neither one of them smoked.

She might well visit the bar again alone, most likely on another quiet, rainy night. When the man was some-where "far away." Kino knew this. The strong light deep within the woman's eyes told him. The woman would sit at the bar, silently drinking a few brandies, waiting for Kino to close up for the night. She would go upstairs, slip off her dress, open her body to him under the light, and show him her new burns. Then the two of them would have sex like a pair of wild animals again. On and on, no time to think, until dawn began to break. Kino didn't know when it would happen, but felt sure it would, *someday*. The woman would decide that. The thought made his throat dry, the kind of dryness no amount of water could quench.

At the end of the summer, Kino's divorce was finalized, and at her lawyer's request, he and his wife met at his bar one afternoon, before it opened, to take care of a few last matters.

The legal issues were quickly settled (Kino didn't contest any of the terms), and the two of them signed the necessary documents and affixed their seals. Kino's wife was wearing a new blue dress, her hair cut shorter than he'd ever seen it. She looked healthy and cheerful. She'd begun a new, no doubt more fulfilling, life. She glanced around the bar. "What a wonderful place," she said. "Quiet, clean, and calm—very you." A short silence followed. *But there's nothing here that really moves you:* Kino imagined that these were the words she wanted to say.

"Would you like something to drink?" he asked.

"A little red wine, if you have some."

Kino took out two wineglasses and poured some Napa Zinfandel. They drank in silence. They weren't about to toast to their divorce. The cat padded over and, surprisingly, leaped into Kino's lap. Kino petted it behind its ears.

"I need to apologize to you," his wife said finally.

"For what?" Kino asked.

"For hurting you," she said. "You were hurt, a little, weren't you?"

"I suppose so," Kino said, after giving it some thought. "I'm human, after all. I was hurt. But whether it was a lot or a little I can't say."

"I wanted to see you and tell you I'm sorry."

Kino nodded. "You've apologized, and I've accepted your apology. No need to worry about it anymore."

"I wanted to tell you what was going on, but I just couldn't find the words."

"But wouldn't we have arrived at the same place, anyway?"

"I guess so," his wife said. "But I hesitated, not saying anything, and we wound up here, at this awful point."

Kino said nothing, and took a sip of wine. Actually, he was starting to forget all that had happened back then. He couldn't recall events in the order they'd occurred. It was like a mixed-up jigsaw puzzle in his mind.

"It's nobody's fault," he said. "I shouldn't have come home a day early. Or I should have let you know I was coming. Then we wouldn't have had to go through that."

His wife didn't say anything.

"When did you start seeing that guy?" Kino asked.

"I don't think we should get into that."

"Better for me not to know, you mean."

His wife said nothing.

"Maybe you're right about that," Kino admitted. He kept on petting the cat, which purred deeply. Another first.

"Maybe I don't have the right to say this," this woman—his former wife—said, "but I think it'd be good for you to forget about what happened and find someone new."

"Maybe," Kino said.

"I know there must be a woman out there who's right for you. It shouldn't be that hard to find her. I wasn't able to be that person for you, and I did a terrible thing. I feel awful about it. But there was something wrong between us from the start, as if we'd done the buttons up wrong. I think you should be able to have a more normal, happy life."

Done the buttons up wrong, Kino thought.

He looked at the new blue dress she was wearing. They were sitting facing each other, so he couldn't tell if there was a zipper or buttons at the back. But he couldn't help thinking about what he would see if he unzipped or unbuttoned her clothes. Her body was no longer his, though. No longer could he see it, let alone touch it. All he could do was imagine it. When he closed his eyes, he saw countless dark brown burn marks wriggling on her pure-white back, like a swarm of worms. He shook his head to dispel that image, and his wife seemed to misinterpret this.

She gently laid her hand on top of his. "I'm sorry," she said. "I'm truly sorry."

Fall came, and the cat disappeared. Then the snakes started to show up.

It took a few days for Kino to realize that it was gone. This female cat—still nameless—came to the bar when it wanted to and sometimes didn't show up for a while. Cats value their freedom. The cat also seemed to be fed somewhere else, too, so if Kino didn't see it for a week, or even ten days, he wasn't particularly worried. But when two weeks passed he began to get concerned. Had it been in an accident? After three weeks Kino's gut told him the cat would never return.

He was fond of the cat, and the cat seemed to trust him. He fed it, provided it a place to sleep, but otherwise let it be. The cat rewarded him by being friendly, or at least not hostile, to him. It was also like a good-luck charm for the bar. Kino had the distinct impression that as long as it was asleep in a corner nothing bad would happen.

Around the time that the cat disappeared, Kino started to notice snakes outside, near the building.

The first snake he saw was dull brown and long. It was in the shade of the willow tree in the front yard, leisurely slithering along. Kino, a bag of groceries in hand, was unlocking the door when he spotted it. It was rare to see a snake in the middle of Tokyo. He was a bit surprised, but he didn't worry about it. Behind his building was the Nezu Museum, with its large gardens. It wasn't inconceivable that a snake might be living there.

But two days later, as he opened the door just before noon to retrieve the paper, he saw a different snake in the same spot. This one was bluish, smaller than the other one, and slimy looking. When the snake saw Kino, it stopped, raised its head slightly, and stared at him. (Or at least looked like it was staring.) Kino hesitated, unsure what to do, and the snake slowly lowered its head and vanished into the shade. The whole thing made him uneasy, as if that snake *knew* him.

It was three days after this, in almost the exact same spot, when he spied the third snake. It was also under the willow tree in the front yard. This snake was considerably smaller than the others and blackish. Kino knew nothing about snakes, but this one struck him as the most dangerous. It looked poisonous, somehow, though he couldn't be sure. He only saw it for a split second. The instant it sensed his presence it burst away, disappearing into the weeds. Three snakes within the space of a week, no matter how you considered it, was too many. Something strange was going on.

Kino phoned his aunt in Izu. After bringing her up to date on neighborhood goings-on, he asked if she had ever seen snakes around the house in Aoyama.

"Snakes?" his aunt said loudly, in surprise. Kino told her about seeing three snakes, one after another, in the front yard.

"I lived there for a long time but can't recall ever seeing any snakes," his aunt said.

"Then seeing three snakes around the house in a week's time is kind of unusual?"

"I would say so. I wonder if it's a sign of an earthquake or something. Animals sense disasters coming and start to act strange."

"If that's true, then maybe I'd better stock up on emergency rations," Kino said.

"That might be a good idea. Tokyo's going to get hit with a huge earthquake someday."

"But are snakes that sensitive to earthquakes?"

"I don't know what they're sensitive to," his aunt said. Kino, of course, didn't know either.

"But snakes are smart creatures," his aunt said. "In ancient legends, they often help guide people. You find this in legends from different cultures all over the world. But when a snake leads you, you don't know whether it's taking you in a good direction or a bad one. In most cases, it's a combination of good and evil."

"It's ambiguous," Kino said.

"Exactly. Snakes are essentially ambiguous creatures. In these legends, the biggest, smartest snake hides its heart somewhere outside its body, so that it doesn't get killed. If you want to kill that snake, you need to go to its hideout when it's not there, locate the beating heart, and cut it in two. Not an easy task, for sure."

How did his aunt know all this?

"The other day I was watching a show on NHK comparing different legends around the world," she explained, "and a professor from some university was talking about this. TV can be pretty useful—when you have time, you ought to watch more TV. Don't underestimate it."

Seeing three snakes in one week's time wasn't normal—that much at least was clear from talking with his aunt.

He would close the bar at midnight, then lock up and go upstairs. Take a bath, read for a while, then turn out the light just before two to go to sleep. Kino began to feel as if the house were surrounded by snakes. He sensed their quiet presence. At midnight, when he closed the bar, the neighborhood was still, with no sound other than the occasional ambulance siren. So quiet he could almost hear a snake slithering along. He took a board and nailed shut the pet door he'd built for the cat, so that no snakes would get inside the house.

At this point, at least, it didn't seem like the snakes planned to harm Kino. They had merely surrounded the little house, silently, ambiguously. Perhaps that was why the gray female cat no longer came by. The woman with the burn scars, too, didn't show up. Kino feared she would appear again, alone, some rainy night. Yet a part of him hoped she would. Another case of ambiguity.

．　　．　　．

One night, just before ten, Kamita appeared. He had a beer, followed by his usual double White Label, and ate a stuffed-cabbage dish. It was unusual for him to come by so late, and stay so long. Occasionally, he glanced up from his reading to stare at the wall in front of him, as if pondering something. As closing time approached, he remained, until he was the last customer.

"Mr. Kino," Kamita said rather formally, after he'd paid his bill. "I find it very regrettable that it's come to this."

"Come to this?" Kino repeated.

"That you'll have to close the bar. Even if only temporarily."

Kino stared at Kamita, not knowing how to respond. Close the bar?

Kamita glanced around the deserted bar, then turned back to Kino. "You haven't quite grasped what I'm saying, have you?"

"I don't think I have."

"I really liked this bar a lot," Kamita said, as if confiding in him. "It was quiet, so I could read, and I enjoyed the music. I was very happy when you opened the bar here. Unfortunately, though, there are some things missing."

"Missing?" Kino said. He had no idea what this could mean. All he could picture was a teacup with a tiny chip in its rim.

"That gray cat won't be coming back," Kamita said. "For the time being, at least."

"Because this place is missing something?"

Kamita didn't reply.

Kino followed Kamita's gaze, and looked carefully

around the bar, but saw nothing out of the ordinary. He did, though, get a sense that the place felt emptier than ever, lacking vitality and color. Something beyond the usual, just-closed-for-the-night feeling.

Kamita spoke up. "Mr. Kino, you're not the type who would willingly do something wrong. I know that very well. But there are times in this world when it's not enough just not to do the wrong thing. Some people use that blank space as a kind of loophole. Do you understand what I'm saying?"

Kino didn't understand.

"Think it over carefully," Kamita said, gazing straight into Kino's eyes. "It's a very important question, worth some serious thought. Though the answer may not come all that easily."

"You're saying that some serious trouble has occurred, not because I did something wrong but because I didn't do the right thing? Some trouble concerning this bar, or me?"

Kamita nodded. "You could put it that way. But I'm not blaming just you, Mr. Kino. I'm at fault, too, for not having noticed it earlier. I should have been paying more attention. This was a comfortable place not just for me but for anybody."

"Then what should I do?" Kino asked.

Kamita was silent, hands stuck in the pockets of his raincoat. Then he spoke. "Close the bar for a while and go far away. There's nothing else you can do at this point. If you know any good priest, you might have him recite some sutras for you, and hang talismans around your house. Though it's hard to find someone like that these days. But I think it's best for you to leave before we have another long spell of rain. Excuse me for asking, but do you have enough money to take a long trip?"

"I guess I could cover it for a while."

"Good. You can worry about what comes after that when you get to that point."

"Who are you, anyway?"

"I'm just a guy named Kamita," Kamita said. "Written with the characters for *kami*, 'god,' and 'field,' but not read as 'Kanda.' I've lived around here for a long time."

Kino decided to plunge ahead and ask. "Mr. Kamita, I have a question. Have you seen snakes around here before?"

Kamita didn't respond. "Here's what you do. Go far away, and don't stay in one place for long. And every Monday and Thursday make sure to send a postcard. Then I'll know you're okay."

"A postcard?"

"Any kind of picture postcard of where you are."

"But who should I address it to?"

"You can mail it to your aunt in Izu. Do not write your own name or any message whatsoever. Just put the address you're sending it to. This is very important, so don't forget."

Kino looked at him in surprise. "You know my aunt?"

"Yes, I know her quite well. Actually, she asked me to keep an eye on you, to make sure that nothing bad happened. Seems like I fell down on the job, though."

Who in the world is this man? Kino asked himself, but there was no way for him to know.

"Mr. Kino, when I know that it's all right for you to return I'll get in touch with you. Until then, stay away from here. Do you understand?"

．　　．　　．

That night, Kino packed for the trip. *It's best for you to leave before we have another long spell of rain.* The announcement was so sudden, and its logic eluded him. But he trusted what Kamita had told him. Kamita's words had a strange persuasive power that went beyond logic. Kino didn't doubt him. He stuffed some clothes and toiletries into a medium-sized shoulder bag, the same bag he'd used on business trips. He knew exactly what he needed and what not to take with him for a long trip.

As dawn came, he pinned a notice to the front door: "Our apologies, but the bar will be closed for the time being." Far away, Kamita had told him. But where he should actually go he had no idea. Should he head north? Or south? He didn't even know which direction. He decided that he would start by retracing a route he often used to take when he was selling running shoes. He boarded a highway express bus and went to Takamatsu. He would make one circuit of Shikoku and then head over to Kyushu.

He checked into a business hotel near Takamatsu Station and stayed there for three days. He wandered around the town and went to see a few movies. The cinemas were deserted during the day, and the movies were, without exception, mind-numbing. When it got dark, he returned to his room and switched on the TV. He followed his aunt's advice and watched educational programs, but got no useful information from them. The second day in Takamatsu was a Thursday, so he bought a postcard at a convenience store, affixed a stamp, and mailed it to his aunt. As Kamita had instructed him, he wrote only her name and address.

On the third night he suddenly decided to sleep with a prostitute. A taxi driver gave him the phone number of a girl to call. She was young, around twenty, with a sleek, beautiful body. But sex with her was, from start to finish, stale and dreary. He did it just to purge himself of lust, but instead it left him with an even greater thirst. "Think it over carefully," Kamita had told him. "It's a very important question, worth some serious thought." But, no matter how seriously he considered it, Kino couldn't work out what the problem was.

It rained that night. Not a strong rain, but a typical autumn rain that didn't show any signs of letting up. Like a monotonous confession, there was no break, no variation. He no longer could even recall when it had begun. The rain brought with it a feeling of cold, damp helplessness. He couldn't even bring himself to grab an umbrella and go out to eat dinner somewhere. He would rather go without eating. The window next to his bed was streaked with water drops, a ceaseless cycle of new drops replacing the old. Kino sat there, endlessly observing the fine transformation in the patterns on the glass. Beyond these patterns lay the random, dark cityscape. He poured himself some whiskey from a pocket flask, added an equal amount of water, and drank it. He had no ice. There was a machine down the hall, but he couldn't even rouse himself to go there. The warmth of the drink fit his listlessness perfectly.

Kino was staying at a cheap business hotel near Kumamoto Station, in Kyushu. Low ceiling, narrow, cramped bed, tiny TV set, minuscule bathtub, crummy little fridge. Everything in the room seemed miniature, and he felt like some awkward, bumbling giant. Still, except for a trip to a nearby convenience store, he stayed holed up in the room all day. At the store, he purchased a small flask of whiskey, some mineral water, and some crackers to snack on. He lay on his bed, reading. When he got tired of reading, he watched TV. When he got tired of watching TV, he read.

It was his third day in Kumamoto now. He still had money in his savings account and, if he'd wanted to, he could have stayed in a much better hotel. But he felt that, for him, just now, this was the right place. If he stayed in a small space like this, he wouldn't have to do any unnecessary thinking, and everything he needed was within reach. He was unexpectedly grateful for this. All he wished for was some music. Teddy Wilson, Vic Dickenson, Buck Clayton—sometimes he longed desperately to listen to their old-time jazz, with its steady, dependable technique and its straightforward chords. He wanted to feel the pure joy they had in performing, their wonderful optimism. That was the kind of music Kino sought, music that no longer existed. But his record collection was far away. He pictured his bar, quiet since he'd closed it. The alleyway, the large willow tree. People reading the sign he'd posted and leaving. What about the cat? If it came back, it would find its door boarded up. And were the snakes still silently encircling the house?

Straight across from his eighth-floor window was the window of a narrow, cheaply built office. From morning till evening, he watched people working there. Here and there the blinds were drawn and he could only catch fragmentary glimpses of what went on, and he had no idea what kind of business it was. Men in ties would pop in and out, while women tapped away at computer keyboards, answered the phone, filed documents. Not exactly the sort of scene to draw one's interest. The features and the clothes of the people working there were ordinary, banal even. Kino watched them for hours for one simple reason: he had nothing else to do. And he found it unexpected, surprising, how happy the people sometimes looked. Some of them occasionally burst out laughing. Why? Working all day in such an unglamorous office, doing things that (at least to Kino's eyes) seemed totally uninspired—how could they do that and still feel so happy? Was there some secret hidden there that he couldn't comprehend? The thought made Kino anxious.

It was about time for him to move on again. Don't stay in one place for long, Kamita had told him. Yet somehow Kino couldn't bring himself to leave this cramped little Kumamoto hotel. He couldn't think of anywhere he wanted to go. The world was a vast ocean with no landmarks, Kino a little boat that had lost its chart and its anchor. When he spread open the map of Kyushu, wondering where to go next, he felt nauseated, as if seasick. He lay down in bed and read a book, glancing up now and then to watch the people in the office across the way. As time passed his body seemed lighter, his skin more transparent.

The day before was a Monday, so he'd bought a postcard in the hotel gift shop with a picture of Kumamoto Castle, written his aunt's name and address, and slapped on a stamp. He held the postcard for a while, vacantly gazing at the castle. A stereotypical photo, the kind you expect to see on a postcard: the castle keep towering grandly in front of a blue sky and puffy white clouds. "Also known as the Gingko Castle, it is one of the three most famous castles in Japan," the caption read. No matter how long he looked at the photo, Kino could find no point of contact between himself and that castle. Then, on an impulse, he turned the postcard over and wrote a message to his aunt:

How are you? How is your back these days?
As you can see, I'm still traveling around by
myself. Sometimes I feel like I'm half transparent.
As if you could see right through to my internal
organs, like a freshly caught squid. Other than
that, I'm doing okay. I hope to visit sometime.
Kino

Kino wasn't at all sure what had motivated him to write that. Kamita had strictly forbidden it. "Do not write your own name or any message whatsoever," Kamita had cautioned him. "Just write the address you're mailing it to. This is very important, so don't forget." But Kino couldn't restrain himself. I have to somehow get connected to reality again, he thought, or else I won't be me anymore. I'll become a man who doesn't exist. Almost automatically, Kino's hand filled the small space on the postcard with tiny, fine printing. And, before he could change his mind, he hurried out to a mailbox near the hotel and slipped the postcard inside.

When he awoke, the clock next to his bed showed two fifteen. Someone was knocking on his door. Not a loud knock but a firm, compact sound, like that of a skilled carpenter pounding a nail. And whoever it was doing the knocking knew that the sound was reaching Kino's ears. The sound dragged Kino out of a deep sleep until his consciousness was thoroughly, even cruelly, clear.

Kino knew who was knocking. The knocking wanted him to get out of bed and open the door. Forcefully, persistently. The person didn't have the strength to open the door from the outside. The door had to be opened by Kino's own hand, from the inside.

It struck him that this visit was exactly what he'd been hoping for, yet, at the same time, what he'd been fearing above all. The ambiguous ambiguity was precisely this, holding on to an empty space between two extremes. "You were hurt, a little, weren't you?" his wife had asked. "I'm human, after all. I was hurt," he'd replied. But that wasn't true. Half of it, at least, was a lie. I wasn't hurt enough when I should have been, Kino admitted to himself. When I should have felt real pain, I stifled it. I didn't want to take it on, so I avoided facing up to it. Which is why my heart is so empty now. The snakes have grabbed that spot and are trying to hide their coldly beating hearts there.

"This was a comfortable place not just for me but for anybody," Kamita had said. Kino finally understood what he meant.

Kino pulled the covers up, shut his eyes, and covered his ears with his hands, escaping into his own narrow little world. I'm not going to look, not going to listen, he told himself. But he couldn't drown out the sound. Even if he ran to the far corners of the earth and stuffed his ears full of clay, as long as he was still alive, as long as he had a shred of consciousness remaining, those knocks would relentlessly track him down. It wasn't a knocking on a door in a business hotel. It was a knocking on the door to his heart. A person couldn't escape that sound. And there were so many hours until dawn—assuming, of course, that there still was a dawn.

He wasn't sure how much time had passed, but he realized that the knocking had stopped. The room was as hushed as the far side of the moon. Still, Kino remained under the covers. He had to be on his guard. He stayed as quiet as he could, perked up his ears, trying to catch a hint of something ominous in the silence. The being outside his door wouldn't give up that easily. It was in no hurry. The moon wasn't out. Only the withered constellations darkly dotted the sky. The world belonged, for a while longer, to those other beings. They had many different methods. They could get what they wanted in all kinds of ways. The roots of darkness could spread everywhere beneath the earth. Patiently taking their time, searching out weak points, they could break apart the most solid rock.

Finally, as Kino had expected, the knocks began once more. But this time they came from another direction. Much closer than before. Whoever was knocking was right outside the window by his bed. Clinging to the sheer wall of the building, eight stories up, face pressed against the window, *tap-tap-tapping* on the rain-streaked glass. He couldn't picture it any other way.

The knocking kept the same beat. Twice. Then twice again. A short pause, then two more knocks. On and on without stopping. Like the sound of a heart beating with emotion.

The curtain was open. Before he fell asleep, he'd been watching the patterns the raindrops formed on the glass.

Kino could imagine what he'd see now, if he stuck his head outside the covers. No—he couldn't imagine it. He had to extinguish the ability to imagine anything. I shouldn't look at it, he told himself. No matter how empty it may be, this is still my heart. There's still some human warmth in it. Memories, like seaweed wrapped around pilings on the beach, wordlessly waiting for high tide. Emotions that, if cut, would bleed. I can't just let them wander somewhere beyond my understanding.

"It's written with the characters for 'god'—*kami*—and 'field'—'god's field'—but isn't pronounced 'Kanda,' as you might expect. It's pronounced 'Kamita.' I live nearby."

"I'll remember that," the large man had said.

"Good idea. Memories can be helpful," Kamita had said.

A sudden thought struck Kino: that Kamita was somehow connected with the old willow tree in the front yard. The tree that had protected him, and his little house. He didn't grasp how this made sense, exactly, but once the thought took hold of him things fell into place.

Kino pictured the limbs of the tree, covered in green, sagging heavily down, nearly to the ground. In the summer, they provided cool shade to the yard. On rainy days, gold droplets glistened on their soft branches. On windless days the branches were sunk in deep, quiet thought; on windy days they swayed like a restless heart. Tiny birds flew over, screeching at one another, alighting neatly on the thin, supple branches only to take off again. For a moment after they flew away, the branches swayed back and forth, delightfully.

Under the covers, Kino curled up like a worm, shut his eyes tight, and thought of the willow. One by one, he pictured its qualities—its color and shape and movements. And he prayed for dawn to come. All he could do was wait like this, patiently, until it grew light out and the birds awoke and began their day. All he could do was trust in the birds, in all the birds, with their wings and beaks. Until then, he couldn't let his heart go blank. That void, the vacuum created by it, would draw them in.

When the willow tree wasn't enough, Kino thought of the slim gray cat, and her fondness for grilled seaweed. He remembered Kamita at the counter, lost in a book, young middle-distance runners going through gruelling repetition drills on a track, the lovely Ben Webster solo on "My Romance" (and the two scratches on the record). *Memories can be helpful.* And he remembered his wife in her new blue dress, her hair trimmed short. He hoped that she was living a healthy, happy life in her new home. Without, he hoped, any wounds on her body. She apologized right to my face, and I accepted that, he thought. I need to learn not just to forget but to forgive.

But the movement of time seemed not to be fixed properly. The bloody weight of desire and the rusty anchor of remorse were blocking its normal flow. Time was not an arrow flying in a straight line. The continuing rain, the confused hands of the clock, the birds still fast asleep, a faceless postal worker silently sorting through postcards, his wife's lovely breasts bouncing violently in the air, something obstinately tapping on the window. As if luring him deeper into a suggestive maze, this ever-regular beat. *Tap tap, tap tap,* then once more—*tap tap.* "Don't look away, look right at it," someone whispered in his ear. "This is what your heart looks like."

The willow branches swayed in the early summer

breeze. In a small dark room, somewhere inside Kino, a warm hand was reaching out to him. Eyes shut, he felt that hand on his, soft and substantial. He'd forgotten this, had been apart from it for far too long. Yes, I am hurt. Very, very deeply. He said this to himself. And he wept. In that dark, still room.

All the while the rain did not let up, drenching the world in a cold chill.

Translated by Philip Gabriel

SAMSA IN LOVE

HE WOKE TO DISCOVER that he had undergone a metamorphosis and become Gregor Samsa.

He lay flat on his back on the bed, looking at the ceiling. It took time for his eyes to adjust to the lack of light. The ceiling seemed to be a common, everyday ceiling of the sort one might find anywhere. Once, it had been painted white, or possibly a pale cream. Years of dust and dirt, however, had given it the color of spoiled milk. It had no ornament, no defining characteristic. No argument, no message. It fulfilled its structural role but aspired to nothing further.

There was a tall window on one side of the room, to his left, but its curtain had been removed and thick boards nailed across the frame. An inch or so of space had been left between the horizontal boards, whether on purpose or not wasn't clear; rays of morning sun shone through, casting a row of bright parallel lines on the floor. Why was the window barricaded in such a rough fashion? Was a major storm or tornado in the offing? Or was it to keep someone from getting in? Or to prevent someone (him, perhaps?) from leaving?

Still on his back, he slowly turned his head and examined the rest of the room. He could see no furniture, apart from the bed on which he lay. No chest of drawers, no desk, no chair. No painting, clock, or mirror on the walls. No lamp or light. Nor could he make out any rug or carpet on the floor. Just bare wood. The walls were covered with wallpaper of a complex design, but it was so old and faded that in the weak light it was next to impossible to make out what the design was.

There was a door to his right, on the wall opposite the window. Its brass knob was discolored in places. It appeared that the room had once served as a normal bedroom. Yet now all vestiges of human life had been stripped away. The only thing that remained was his solitary bed in the center. And it had no bedding. No sheets, no coverlet, no pillow. Just an ancient mattress.

Samsa had no idea where he was, or what he should do. All he knew was that he was now a human whose name was Gregor Samsa. And how did he know *that*? Perhaps someone had whispered it in his ear while he lay sleeping? But who had he been before he became Gregor Samsa? *What* had he been?

The moment he began contemplating that question, however, something like a black column of mosquitoes swirled up in his head. The column grew thicker and denser as it moved to a softer part of his brain, buzzing all the way. Samsa decided to stop thinking. Trying to think anything through at this point was too great a burden.

In any case, he had to learn how to move his body. He

couldn't lie there staring up at the ceiling forever. The posture left him much too vulnerable. He had no chance of surviving an attack—by predatory birds, for example. As a first step, he tried to move his fingers. There were ten of them, long things affixed to his two hands. Each was equipped with a number of joints, which made synchronizing their movements very complicated. To make matters worse, his body felt numb, as though it were immersed in a sticky, heavy liquid, so that it was difficult to send strength to his extremities.

Nevertheless, after repeated attempts and failures, by closing his eyes and focusing his mind he was able to bring his fingers more under control. Little by little, he was learning how to make them work together. As his fingers became operational, the numbness that had enveloped his body withdrew. In its place—like a dark and sinister reef revealed by a retreating tide—came an excruciating pain.

It took Samsa some time to realize that the pain was hunger. This ravenous desire for food was new to him, or at least he had no memory of experiencing anything like it. It was as if he had not had a bite to eat for a week. As if the center of his body were now a cavernous void. His bones creaked; his muscles clenched; his organs twitched.

Unable to withstand the pain any longer, Samsa put his elbows on the mattress and, bit by bit, pushed himself up. His spine emitted several low and sickening cracks in the process. My goodness, Samsa thought, how long have I been lying here? His body protested each move. But he struggled through, marshaling his strength, until, at last, he managed to sit up.

Samsa looked down in dismay at his naked body. How ill-formed it was! Worse than ill-formed. It possessed no means of self-defense. Smooth white skin (covered by only a perfunctory amount of hair) with fragile blue blood vessels visible through it; a soft, unprotected belly; ludicrous, impossibly shaped genitals; gangly arms and legs (just two of each!); a scrawny, breakable neck; an enormous, misshapen head with a tangle of stiff hair on its crown; two absurd ears, jutting out like a pair of seashells. *Was this thing really him?* Could a body so preposterous, so easy to destroy (no shell for protection, no weapons for attack), survive in the world? Why hadn't he been turned into a fish? Or a sunflower? A fish or a sunflower made sense. More sense, anyway, than this creature, Gregor Samsa. There was no other way to look at it.

Steeling himself, he lowered his legs over the edge of the bed until the soles of his feet touched the floor. The unexpected cold of the bare wood made him gasp. After several failed attempts that sent him crashing to the floor, at last he was able to balance on his two feet. He stood there, bruised and sore, one hand clutching the frame of the bed for support. His head was inordinately heavy and hard to hold up. Sweat streamed from his armpits, and his genitals shrank from the stress. He had to take several deep breaths before his constricted muscles began to relax.

Once he was used to standing, he had to learn to walk. Walking on two legs amounted to a kind of torture, each movement an exercise in pain. No matter how he looked at it, advancing his right and left legs one after the other was a bizarre proposition that flouted all natural laws, while the precarious distance from his eyes to the ground made him cringe in fear. It took time to learn how to coordinate his hip and knee joints, and even longer to balance their movements. Each time he took a step forward, his knees shook with terror, and he steadied himself against the wall with both hands.

But he knew that he could not remain in this room forever. If he didn't find food, and quickly, his starving belly would consume his own flesh, and he would cease to exist.

He tottered toward the door, pawing at the wall as he went. The journey seemed to take hours, although he had no way of measuring the time, except by the pain. His movements were awkward, his pace snail-like. He couldn't advance without leaning on something for support. On the street, his best hope would be that people saw him as disabled. Yet, despite the discomfort, with each step he was learning how his joints and muscles worked.

He grasped the doorknob and pulled. It didn't budge. A push yielded the same result. Next, he turned the knob to the right and pulled. The door opened partway with a slight squeak. It hadn't been locked. He poked his head through the opening and looked out. The hallway was deserted. It was as quiet as the bottom of the ocean. He extended his left leg through the doorway, swung the upper half of his body out, with one hand on the doorframe, and followed with his right leg. He moved slowly down the corridor in his bare feet, hands on the wall.

There were four doors in the hallway, including the

one he had just used. All were identical, fashioned of the same dark wood. What, or who, lay beyond them? He longed to open them and find out. Perhaps then he might begin to understand the mysterious circumstances in which he found himself. Or at least discover a clue of some sort. Nevertheless, he passed by each of the doors, making as little noise as possible. The need to fill his belly trumped his curiosity. He had to find something substantial to eat, and quickly.

And now he knew where to find that "something substantial."

Just follow the smell, he thought, sniffing. It was the aroma of cooked food, tiny particles that wafted to him through the air. The information gathered by olfactory receptors in his nose was being transmitted to his brain, producing an anticipation so vivid, a craving so violent, that he could feel his innards being slowly twisted, as if by an experienced torturer. Saliva flooded his mouth.

To reach the source of the aroma, however, he would have to go down a steep flight of stairs, seventeen of them. He was having a hard enough time walking on level ground—navigating those steps would be a true nightmare. He grabbed the banister with both hands and began his descent. His skinny ankles felt ready to collapse under his weight, and he almost went tumbling down the steps. When he twisted his body to right him-self his bones and muscles shrieked in pain.

And what was on Samsa's mind as he made his way down the staircase? Fish and sunflowers, for the most part. Had I been transformed into a fish or a sunflower, he thought, I could have lived out my life in peace, without struggling up and down steps like these. Why must I undertake something this perilous and unnatural? It makes no sense—there is no rhyme or reason to it.

When Samsa reached the bottom of the seventeen steps, he pulled himself upright, summoned his remaining strength, and hobbled in the direction of the enticing smell. He crossed the high-ceilinged entrance hall and stepped through the dining room's open doorway. The food was laid out on a large oval table. There were five chairs, but no sign of people. White wisps of steam rose from the serving plates. A glass vase bearing a dozen lilies occupied the center of the table. Four places were set with napkins and cutlery, untouched, by the look of it. It seemed as though people had been sitting down to eat their breakfast a few minutes earlier, when some sudden and unforeseen event sent them all running off.

What had happened? Where had they gone? Or where had they been taken? Would they return to eat their breakfast?

But Samsa had no time to ponder such questions. Falling into the nearest chair, he grabbed whatever food he could reach with his bare hands and stuffed it into his mouth, quite ignoring the knives, spoons, forks, and napkins. He tore bread into pieces and downed it without jam or butter, gobbled fat boiled sausages whole, devoured hard-boiled eggs with such speed that he almost forgot to peel them, scooped up handfuls of still-warm mashed potatoes, and plucked pickles with his fingers. He chewed it all together, and washed the remnants down with water from a jug. Taste was of no consequence. Bland or delicious, spicy or sour—it was all the same to him. What mattered was filling that empty cavern inside him. He ate with total concentration, as if racing against time. He was so fixated on eating that once, as he was licking his fingers, he sank his teeth into them by mistake. Scraps of food flew everywhere, and when a platter fell to the floor and smashed he paid no attention whatsoever.

By the time Samsa had eaten his fill and sat back to catch his breath, almost nothing was left, and the dining table was an awful sight. It looked as if a flock of quarrelsome crows had flown in through an open window, gorged themselves, and flown away again. The only thing untouched was the vase of lilies; had there been less food, he might have devoured them as well. That was how hungry he had been.

He sat, dazed, in his chair for a long while. Hands on the table, he gazed at the lilies through half-closed eyes and took long, slow breaths, while the food he had eaten worked its way through his digestive system, from his esophagus to his intestines. A sense of satiety came over him like a rising tide.

He picked up a metal pot and poured coffee into a white ceramic cup. The pungent fragrance recalled something to him. It did not come directly, however; it arrived in stages. It was a strange feeling, as if he were recollecting the present from the future. As if time had somehow been split in two, so that memory and experience revolved within a closed cycle, each following the other. He poured a liberal amount of cream into his coffee, stirred it with his finger, and drank. Although the coffee had cooled, a slight warmth remained. He held it in his mouth before warily allowing it to trickle down his throat. He found that it calmed him to a degree.

All of a sudden, he felt cold. The intensity of his hunger had blotted out his other senses. Now that he was sated, the morning chill on his skin made him tremble. The fire had gone out. None of the heaters seemed to be turned on. On top of that, he was stark naked—even his feet were bare.

He knew that he had to find something to wear. He was too cold like this. Moreover, his lack of clothes was bound to be an issue should someone appear. There might be a knock at the door. Or the people who had been about to sit down to breakfast a short while before might return. Who knew how they would react if they found him in this state?

He understood all this. He did not surmise it, or perceive it in an intellectual way; he knew it, pure and simple. Samsa had no idea where such knowledge came from. Perhaps it was related to those revolving memories he was having.

He stood up from his chair and walked out to the front hall. He was still awkward, but at least he could stand and walk on two legs without clinging to something. There was a wrought iron umbrella stand in the hall that held several walking sticks. He pulled out a black one made of oak to help him move around; just grasping its sturdy handle relaxed and encouraged him. And now he would have a weapon to fight back with should birds attack. He went to the window and looked out through the crack in the lace curtains.

The house faced onto a street. It was not a very big street. Nor were many people on it. Nevertheless, he noted that every person who passed was fully clothed. The clothes were of various colors and styles. Most were men, but there were one or two women as well. The men and women wore different garments. Shoes of stiff leather covered their feet. A few sported brightly polished boots. He could hear the soles of their footwear clack on the cobblestones. Many of the men and women wore hats. They seemed to think nothing of walking on two legs and keeping their genitals covered. Samsa compared his reflection in the hall's full-length mirror with the people walking outside. The man he saw in the mirror was a shabby, frail-looking creature. His belly was smeared with gravy, and bread crumbs clung to his pubic hair like bits of cotton. He swept the filth away with his hand.

Yes, he thought again, I must find something to cover my body.

He looked out at the street once more, checking for birds. But there were no birds in sight.

The ground floor of the house consisted of the hallway, the dining room, a kitchen, and a living room. As far as he could tell, however, none of those rooms held anything resembling clothes. Which meant that the putting on and taking off of clothing must occur somewhere else. Perhaps in a room on the second floor.

Samsa returned to the staircase and began to climb. He was surprised to discover how much easier it was to go up than to go down. Clutching the railing, he was able to make his way up the seventeen steps at a much faster rate and without undue pain or fear, stopping several times along the way (though never for long) to catch his breath.

One might say that luck was with him, for none of the doors on the second floor were locked. All he had to do was turn the knob and push, and each door swung open. There were four rooms in total, and, apart from the freezing room with the bare floor in which he had woken, all were comfortably furnished. Each had a bed with clean bedding, a dresser, a writing desk, a lamp affixed to the ceiling or the wall, and a rug or a carpet with an intricate pattern. All were tidy and clean. Books were neatly lined up in their cases, and framed oil paintings of landscapes adorned the walls. Each room had a glass vase filled with bright flowers. None had rough boards nailed across the windows. Their windows had lace curtains, through which sunlight poured like a blessing from above. The beds all showed signs of someone's having slept in them. He could see the imprint of heads on pillows.

Samsa found a dressing gown his size in the closet of the largest room. It looked like something he might be able to manage. He hadn't a clue what to do with the other clothes—how to put them on, how to wear them. They were just too complicated: too many buttons, for one thing, and he was unsure how to tell front from back, or top from bottom. Which was supposed to go on the outside, and which underneath? The dressing gown, on the other hand, was simple, practical, and quite free of ornament, the sort of thing he thought he could handle. Its light, soft cloth felt good against his skin, and its color was dark blue. He even turned up a matching pair of slippers.

He pulled the dressing gown over his naked body and, after much trial and error, succeeded in fastening the belt around his waist. He looked in the mirror at himself, clad now in gown and slippers. This was certainly better than walking around naked. Mastering how to wear clothes would require close observation and considerable time. Until then, this gown was the only answer. It wasn't as warm as it might have been, to be sure, but as long as he remained indoors it would stave off the cold. Best of all, he no longer had to worry that his soft skin would be exposed to vicious birds.

When the doorbell rang, Samsa was dozing in the biggest room (and in the biggest bed) in the house. It was warm under the feather quilts, as cozy as if he were sleeping in an egg. He woke from a dream. He couldn't remember it in detail, but it had been pleasant and cheerful. The bell echoing through the house, however, yanked him back to cold reality.

He dragged himself from the bed, fastened his gown, put on his dark blue slippers, grabbed his black walking stick, and, hand on railing, tottered down the stairs. It was far easier than it had been on the first occasion. Still, the danger of falling was ever present. He could not afford to let down his guard. Keeping a close eye on his feet, he picked his way down the stairs one step at a time, as the doorbell continued to ring. Whoever was pushing the buzzer had to be a most impatient and stubborn person.

Walking stick in his left hand, Samsa approached the front door. He twisted the knob to the right and pulled, and the door swung in.

A little woman was standing outside. A very little woman. It was a wonder she was able to reach the buzzer. When he looked more closely, however, he realized that the issue wasn't her size. It was her back, which was bent forward in a perpetual stoop. This made her appear small even though, in fact, her frame was of normal dimensions. She had fastened her hair with a rubber band to prevent it from spilling over her face. The hair was deep chestnut and very abundant. She was dressed in a battered tweed jacket and a full, loose-fitting skirt that covered her ankles. A striped cotton scarf was wrapped around her neck. She wore no hat. Her shoes were of the tall lace-up variety, and she appeared to be in her early twenties. There was still something of the girl about her. Her eyes were big, her nose small, and her lips twisted a little to one side, like a skinny moon. Her dark eyebrows formed two straight lines across her forehead, giving her a skeptical look.

"Is this the Samsa residence?" the woman said, craning her head up to look at him. Then she twisted her body all over. Much the way the earth twists during a violent earthquake.

He was taken aback at first, but pulled himself together. "Yes," he said. Since he was Gregor Samsa, this was likely the Samsa residence. At any rate, there could be no harm in saying so.

Yet the woman seemed to find his answer less than satisfying. A slight frown creased her brow. Perhaps she had picked up a note of confusion in his voice.

"So this is *really* the Samsa residence?" she said in a sharp voice. Like an experienced gatekeeper grilling a shabby visitor.

"I am Gregor Samsa," Samsa said, in as relaxed a tone as possible. Of this, at least, he was sure.

"I hope you're right," she said, reaching down for a cloth bag at her feet. It was black, and seemed very heavy. Worn through in places, it had doubtless had a number of owners. "So let's get started."

She strode into the house without waiting for a reply. Samsa closed the door behind her. She stood there, looking him up and down. It seemed that his gown and slippers had aroused her suspicions.

"I appear to have woken you," she said, her voice cold.

"That's perfectly all right," Samsa replied. He could tell by her dark expression that his clothes were a poor fit for the occasion. "I must apologize for my appearance," he went on. "There are reasons . . ."

The woman ignored this. "So, then?" she said through pursed lips.

"So, then?" Samsa echoed.

"So, then, where is the lock that's causing the problem?" the woman said.

"The lock?"

"The lock that's broken," she said. Her irritation had been evident from the beginning. "You asked us to come and repair it."

"Ah," Samsa said. "The broken lock."

Samsa ransacked his mind. No sooner had he managed to focus on one thing, however, than that black column of mosquitoes rose up again.

"I haven't heard anything in particular about a lock," he said. "My guess is it belongs to one of the doors on the second floor."

The woman glowered at him. "Your guess?" she said, peering up at his face. Her voice had grown even icier. An eyebrow arched in disbelief. "One of the doors?" she went on.

Samsa could feel his face flush. His ignorance regarding the lock struck him as most embarrassing. He cleared his throat to speak, but the words did not come.

"Mr. Samsa, are your parents in? I think it's better if I talk to them."

"They seem to have gone out on an errand," Samsa said.

"An errand?" she said, appalled. "In the midst of these *troubles*?"

"I really have no idea. When I woke up this morning, everyone was gone," Samsa said.

"Good grief," the young woman said. She heaved a long sigh. "We did tell them that someone would come at this time today."

"I'm terribly sorry."

The woman stood there for a moment. Then, slowly, her arched eyebrow descended, and she looked at the black walking stick in Samsa's left hand. "Are your legs bothering you, Gregor Samsa?"

"Yes, a little," he prevaricated.

Once again, the woman writhed suddenly. Samsa had no idea what this action meant or what its purpose was. Yet he was drawn by instinct to the complex sequence of movements.

"Well, what's to be done," the woman said in a tone of resignation. "Let's take a look at those doors on the second floor. I came over the bridge and all the way across town through this terrible upheaval to get here. Risked my life, in fact. So it wouldn't make much sense to say, 'Oh, really, no one is here? I'll come back later,' would it?"

This terrible upheaval? Samsa couldn't grasp what she was talking about. What awful change was taking place? But he decided not to ask for details. Better to avoid exposing his ignorance even further.

Back bent, the young woman took the heavy black

bag in her right hand and toiled up the stairs, much like a crawling insect. Samsa labored after her, his hand on the railing. Her creeping gait aroused his sympathy—it reminded him of something.

The woman stood at the top of the steps and surveyed the hallway. "So," she said, "*one* of these four doors *probably* has a broken lock, right?"

Samsa's face reddened. "Yes," he said. "One of these. It could be the one at the end of the hall on the left, possibly," he said, faltering. This was the door to the bare room in which he had woken that morning.

"*It could be*," the woman said in a voice as lifeless as an extinguished bonfire. "*Possibly.*" She turned around to examine Samsa's face.

"Somehow or other," Samsa said.

The woman sighed again. "Gregor Samsa," she said dryly. "You are a true joy to talk to. Such a rich vocabulary, and you always get to the point." Then her tone changed. "But no matter. Let's check the door on the left at the end of the hall first."

The woman went to the door. She turned the knob back and forth and pushed, and it opened inward. The room was as it had been before: only a bed with a bare mattress that was less than clean. This was the mattress he had woken on that morning as Gregor Samsa. It had been no dream. The floor bare and cold. Boards nailed across the window. The woman must have noticed all this, but she showed no sign of surprise. Her demeanor suggested that similar rooms could be found all over the city.

She squatted down, opened the black bag, pulled out a white flannel cloth, and spread it on the floor. Then she took out a number of tools, which she lined up carefully on the cloth, like an inquisitor displaying the sinister instruments of his trade before some poor martyr.

Selecting a wire of medium thickness, she inserted it into the lock and, with a practiced hand, manipulated it from a variety of angles. Her eyes were narrowed in concentration, her ears alert for the slightest sound. Next, she chose a thinner wire and repeated the process. Her face grew somber, and her mouth twisted into a ruthless shape, like a Chinese sword. She took a large flashlight and, with a black look in her eyes, began to examine the lock in detail.

"Do you have the key for this lock?" she asked Samsa.

"I haven't the slightest idea where the key is," he answered honestly.

"Ah, Gregor Samsa, sometimes you make me want to die," she said.

After that, she quite ignored him. She selected a screwdriver from the tools lined up on the cloth and proceeded to remove the lock from the door. Her movements were slow and cautious. She paused from time to time to twist and writhe about as she had before.

While he stood behind her, watching her move in that fashion, Samsa's own body began to respond in a strange way. He was growing hot all over, and his nostrils were flaring. His mouth was so dry that he produced a loud gulp whenever he swallowed. His earlobes itched. And his sexual organ, which had dangled in such a sloppy way until that point, began to stiffen and expand. As it rose, a bulge developed at the front of his gown. He was in the dark, however, as to what that might signify.

Having extracted the lock, the young woman took it to the window to inspect in the sunlight that shone between the boards. She poked it with a thin wire and gave it a hard shake to see how it sounded, her face glum and her lips pursed. Finally, she sighed again and turned to face Samsa.

"The insides are shot," the woman said. "It's kaput. This is the one, just like you said."

"That's good," Samsa said.

"No, it's not," the woman said. "There's no way I can repair it here on the spot. It's a special kind of lock. I'll have to take it back and let my father or one of my older brothers work on it. They may be able to fix it. I'm just an apprentice—I can only handle regular locks."

"I see," Samsa said. So this young woman had a father and several brothers. A whole family of locksmiths.

"Actually, one of them was supposed to come today, but because of the commotion going on out there they sent me instead. The city is riddled with checkpoints." She looked back down at the lock in her hands. "But how did the lock get broken like this? It's weird. Someone must have gouged out the insides with a special kind of tool. There's no other way to explain it."

Again she writhed. Her arms rotated as if she were a swimmer practicing a new stroke. He found the action mesmerizing and very exciting.

Samsa made up his mind. "May I ask you a question?" he said.

"A question?" she said, casting him a dubious glance. "I can't imagine what, but go ahead."

"Why do you twist about like that every so often?"

She looked at Samsa with her lips slightly parted. "Twist about?" She thought for a moment. "You mean like this?" She demonstrated the motion for him.

"Yes, that's it."

"My brassiere doesn't fit," she said dourly. "That's all."

"Brassiere?" Samsa said in a dull voice. It was a word he couldn't call up from his memory.

"A brassiere. You know what that is, don't you?" the woman said. "Or do you find it strange that hunchback women wear brassieres? Do you think it's presumptuous of us?"

"Hunchback?" Samsa said. Yet another word that was sucked into that vast emptiness he carried within. He had no idea what she was talking about. Still, he knew that he should say something.

"No, I don't think so at all," he mumbled.

"Listen up. We hunchbacks have two breasts, just like other women, and we have to use a brassiere to support them. We can't walk around like cows with our udders swinging."

"Of course not." Samsa was lost.

"But brassieres aren't designed for us—they get loose. We're built differently from regular women, right? So we have to twist around every so often to put them back in place. Hunchbacks have more problems than you can imagine. Is that why you've been staring at me from behind? Is that how you get your kicks?"

"No, not at all. I was just curious why you were doing that."

So, he inferred, a brassiere was an apparatus designed to hold the breasts in place, and a hunchback was a person with this woman's particular build. There was so much in this world that he had to learn.

"Are you sure you're not making fun of me?" the woman asked.

"I'm not making fun of you."

The woman cocked her head and looked up at Samsa. She could tell that he was speaking the truth—there didn't seem to be any malice in him. He was just a little weak in the head, that was all. Age about thirty. As well as being lame, he seemed to be intellectually challenged. But he was from a good family, and his manners were impeccable. He was nice-looking, too, but thin as a rail with too-big ears and a pasty complexion.

It was then that she noticed the protuberance pushing out the lower part of his gown.

"What the hell is that?" she said stonily. "What's that *bulge* doing there?"

Samsa looked down at the front of his gown. His organ was really very swollen. He could surmise from her tone that its condition was somehow inappropriate.

"I get it," she spat out. "You're wondering what it would be like to fuck a hunchback, aren't you?"

"Fuck?" he said. One more word he couldn't place.

"You imagine that, since a hunchback is bent at the waist, you can just take her from the rear with no problem, right?" the woman said. "Believe me, there are lots of perverts like you around, who seem to think that we'll let you do what you want because we're hunchbacks. Well, think again, buster. We're not that easy!"

"I'm very confused," Samsa said. "If I have displeased you in some way, I am truly sorry. I apologize. Please forgive me. I meant no harm. I've been unwell, and there are so many things I don't understand."

"All right, I get the picture." She sighed. "You're a little *slow*, right? But your wiener is in great shape. Those are the breaks, I guess."

"I'm sorry," Samsa said again.

"Forget it." She relented. "I've got four no-good brothers at home, and since I was a little girl they've shown me everything. They treat it like a big joke. *Mean* buggers, all of them. So I'm not kidding when I say I know the score."

She squatted to put her tools back in the bag, wrapping the broken lock in the flannel and gently placing it alongside.

"I'm taking the lock home with me," she said, standing up. "Tell your parents. We'll either fix it or replace it. If we have to get a new one, though, it may take some time, things being the way they are. Don't forget to tell them, okay? Do you follow me? Will you remember?"

"I'll tell them," Samsa said.

She walked slowly down the staircase, Samsa trailing behind. They made quite a study in contrasts: she looked as if she were crawling on all fours, while he tilted backward in a most unnatural way. Yet their pace was identical. Samsa was trying hard to quell his "bulge," but the thing just wouldn't return to its former state. Watching her movements from behind as she descended the stairs made his heart pound. Hot, fresh blood coursed through his veins. The stubborn bulge persisted.

"As I told you before, my father or one of my brothers was supposed to come today," the woman said when they reached the front door. "But the streets are crawling with soldiers and tanks. There are checkpoints on all the bridges, and people are being rounded up. That's why the men in my family can't go out. Once you get arrested, there's no telling when you'll return. That's why I was sent. All the way across Prague, alone. 'No one will notice a hunchbackgirl,' they said."

"Tanks?" Samsa murmured.

"Yeah, lots of them. Tanks with cannons and machine guns. Your cannon is impressive," she said, pointing at the bulge beneath his gown, "but these cannons are bigger and harder, and a lot more lethal. Let's hope everyone in your family makes it back safely. You honestly have no clue where they went, do you?"

Samsa shook his head no. He had no idea.

Samsa decided to take the bull by the horns. "Would it be possible to meet again?" he said.

The young woman craned her head at Samsa. "Are you saying you want to see me again?"

"Yes. I want to see you one more time."

"With your thing sticking out like that?"

Samsa looked down again at the bulge. "I don't know how to explain it, but that has nothing to do with my feelings. It must be some kind of heart problem."

"No kidding," she said, impressed. "A heart problem, you say. That's an interesting way to look at it. Never heard that one before."

"You see, it's out of my control."

"And it has nothing to do with fucking?"

"Fucking isn't on my mind. Really."

"So let me get this straight. When your thing grows big and hard like that, it's not your mind but your heart that's causing it?"

Samsa nodded in assent.

"Swear to God?" the woman said.

"God," Samsa echoed. Another word he couldn't remember having heard before. He fell silent.

The woman gave a weary shake of her head. She twisted and turned again to adjust her brassiere. "Forget it. It seems God left Prague a few days ago. Let's forget about Him."

"So can I see you again?" Samsa asked.

The girl raised an eyebrow. A new look came over her face—her eyes seemed fixed on some distant and misty landscape. "You really want to see me again?"

Samsa nodded.

"What would we do?"

"We could talk together."

"About what?" the woman asked.

"About lots of things."

"Just talk?"

"There is so much I want to ask you," Samsa said.

"About what?"

"About this world. About you. About me."

The young woman thought for a moment. "So it's not all about you shoving *that* in me?"

"No, not at all," Samsa said without hesitation. "I feel like there are so many things we need to talk about. Tanks, for example. And God. And brassieres. And locks."

Another silence fell over the two of them.

"I don't know," the woman said at last. She shook her head slowly, but the chill in her voice was less noticeable. "You're better brought up than me. And I doubt your parents would be thrilled to see their precious son involved with a hunchback from the wrong side of town. Even if that son is lame and a little slow. On top of that, our city is overflowing with foreign tanks and troops. Who knows what lies ahead."

Samsa certainly had no idea what lay ahead. He was in the dark about everything: the future, of course, but the present and the past as well. What was right, and what was wrong? Just learning how to dress was a riddle.

"At any rate, I'll come back this way in a few days," the hunchbacked young woman said. "If we can fix it, I'll bring the lock, and if we can't I'll return it to you anyway. You'll be charged for the service call, of course. If you're here, then we can see each other. Whether we'll be able to have that long talk or not I don't know. But if I were you I'd keep that bulge hidden from your parents. In the real world, you don't get compliments for exposing that kind of thing."

Samsa nodded. He wasn't at all clear, though, how that kind of thing could be kept out of sight.

"It's strange, isn't it?" the woman said in a pensive voice. "Everything is blowing up around us, but there are still those who care about a broken lock, and others who are dutiful enough to try to fix it . . . But maybe that's the way it should be. Maybe working on the little things as dutifully and honestly as we can is how we stay sane when the world is falling apart."

The woman looked up at Samsa's face. She raised one of her eyebrows. "I don't mean to pry, but what was going on in that room on the second floor? Why did your parents need such a big lock for a room that held nothing but a bed, and why did it bother them so much when the lock got broken? And what about those boards nailed across the window? Was something locked up in there—is that it?"

Samsa shook his head. If someone or something had been shut up in there, it must have been him. But why had that been necessary? He hadn't a clue.

"I guess there's no point in asking you," the woman said. "Well, I've got to go. They'll worry about me if I'm late. Pray that I make it across town in one piece. That the soldiers will overlook a poor little hunchbacked girl. That none of them is perverted. We're being fucked over enough as it is."

"I will pray," Samsa said. But he had no idea what "perverted" meant. Or "pray," for that matter.

The woman picked up her black bag and, still bent over, headed for the door.

"Will I see you again?" Samsa asked one last time.

"If you think of someone enough, you're sure to meet them again," she said in parting. This time there was real warmth in her voice.

"Look out for birds," he called after her. She turned and nodded. Then she walked out to the street.

Samsa watched through the crack in the curtains as her hunched form set off across the cobblestones. She moved awkwardly but with surprising speed. He found her every gesture charming. She reminded him of a water strider that had left the water to scamper about on dry land. As far as he could tell, walking the way she did made a lot more sense than wobbling around upright on two legs.

She had not been out of sight long when he noticed that his genitals had returned to their soft and shrunken state. That brief and violent bulge had, at some point, vanished. Now his organ dangled between his legs like an innocent fruit, peaceful and defenseless. His balls rested comfortably in their sac. Readjusting the belt of his gown, he sat down at the dining room table and drank what remained of his cold coffee.

The people who lived here had gone somewhere else. He didn't know who they were, but he imagined that they were his family. Something had happened all of a sudden, and they had left. Perhaps they would never return. What did "the world is falling apart" mean? Gregor

Samsa had no idea. Foreign troops, checkpoints, tanks—everything was wrapped in mystery.

The only thing he knew for certain was that he wanted to see that hunchbacked girl again. To sit face-to-face and talk to his heart's content. To unravel the riddles of the world with her. He wanted to watch from every angle the way she twisted and writhed when she adjusted her brassiere. If possible, he wanted to run his hands over her body. To touch her soft skin and feel her warmth with his fingertips. To walk side by side with her up and down the staircases of the world.

Just thinking about her made him warm inside. No longer did he wish to be a fish or a sunflower—or anything else, for that matter. For sure, it was a great inconvenience to have to walk on two legs and wear clothes and eat with a knife and fork. There were so many things he didn't know. Yet had he been a fish or a sunflower, and not a human being, he might never have experienced this emotion. So he felt.

Samsa sat there for a long time with his eyes closed. Then, making up his mind, he stood, grabbed his black walking stick, and headed for the stairs. He would return to the second floor and figure out the proper way to dress. For now, at least, that would be his mission.

The world was waiting for him to learn.

Translated by Ted Goossen

MEN WITHOUT WOMEN

THE CALL CAME IN AFTER ONE A.M. and woke me up. Phones ringing in the middle of the night always sound harsh and grating, like some savage metal tool out to destroy the world. I felt it was my duty, as a member of the human race, to put a stop to it, so I got out of bed, padded over to the living room, and picked up the receiver.

A man's low voice informed me that a woman had vanished from this world forever. The voice belonged to the woman's husband. At least that's what he said. And he went on. My wife committed suicide last Wednesday, he said. In any case, I thought I should let you know. *In any case.* As far as I could make out, there was not a drop of emotion in his voice. It was like he was reading lines meant for a telegram, with barely any space at all between each word. An announcement, pure and simple. Unadorned reality. Period.

What did I say in response? I must have said something, but I can't recall. At any rate, there was a prolonged period of silence. Like a deep hole in the middle of the road that the two of us were staring into from opposite sides. Then, without a word, as if he were gently placing a fragile piece of artwork on the floor, the man hung up. I stood there, in a white T-shirt and blue boxers, pointlessly clutching the phone.

How did he know about me? I had no idea. Had she mentioned my name to her husband, as an old boyfriend? But why? And how did he know my phone number (which was unlisted)? In the first place, why *me*? Why would her husband go to the trouble of calling me to let me know his wife had died? I couldn't imagine she'd left a request like that in a farewell note. We'd broken up years earlier. And we'd never seen each other since—not even once. We had never even talked on the phone.

That's neither here nor there. The bigger problem was that he didn't explain a single thing to me. He thought he needed to let me know his wife had killed herself. And somehow he'd gotten hold of my phone number. Beyond that, though—nothing. It seemed his intention was to leave me stuck somewhere in the middle, dangling between knowledge and ignorance. But why? To get me thinking about something?

Like *what*?

I was clueless. The number of question marks had only multiplied, like a child making rubber-stamp marks all over a page in a notebook.

So I still don't know why she killed herself, or how she did it. Even if I wanted to inquire, there was no way to do so. I had no idea where she lived, and frankly I hadn't even known she was married. So I didn't know her married name (and the man on the phone hadn't given his name). How long had they been married? Did they have a child—or children?

Still, I accepted what her husband had told me. I didn't feel like doubting it. After she left me, she had continued to live on in this world, likely fell in love with somebody else, married him, and last Wednesday—for whatever reason and by whatever means—she had ended her life. *In any case.* There was certainly something in the man's voice that linked him deeply to the world of the dead. In the late-night stillness, I could hear that connection, and catch a glint from that taut thread. So calling me like that, after one in the morning—whether intentional or not—had been the right decision. If he'd called at one in the afternoon, I never would have sensed this.

By the time I put down the phone and shuffled back to bed, my wife was awake.

"What was that call about? Did somebody die?" my wife asked.

"Nobody died. It was a wrong number," I said, my voice slow and sleepy.

My wife, of course, didn't buy it, for my own voice was now tinged with the dead too. The kind of unsettled feeling the newly deceased bring on is highly contagious. It moves through the phone line as a faint trembling, transforming the sound of words, bringing the world in sync with its vibration. But my wife said no more. The two of us lay there in the dark, listening carefully to the silence, each of us lost in our own thoughts.

This woman was the third woman I'd gone out with who'd killed herself. If you think about it—and you don't really need to, since it's obvious—this is an extremely high fatality rate. I couldn't believe it. I hadn't gone out with that many women in my life. Why these women, all still young, had taken their lives, or felt *compelled* to take their lives, was beyond my comprehension. I hoped it wasn't because of me, or in some way connected with me. And I hoped they hadn't assumed I would serve as a witness to their deaths. Deep down, I prayed this was the case. And—how should I put it?—this woman, the third woman (not having a name to call her by makes things awkward, so I'll call her "M")—wasn't the type to commit suicide. Far from it. I mean, she had all the brawny sailors in the world protecting her, watching out for her.

I can't give any particulars about what kind of woman M was, or how we met, or what we did together. If the facts came out, they might cause trouble for people who are still alive. So all I can write here is that a long time ago she and I were very close, and at a certain point we broke up.

Truthfully I like to think of M as a girl I met when she was fourteen. That didn't actually happen, but here, at least, I'd like to imagine it did. We met when we were fourteen in a junior high classroom. It was biology class, as I recall. Something about ammonites and coelacanths. She was in the seat next to mine. "I forgot my eraser," I told her, "so if you have an extra, could you let me borrow it?" She took her eraser, broke it in two, and gave me half. And smiled broadly. Like the saying goes, in that instant I fell in love. She was the most beautiful girl I'd ever seen. At least that's what I felt at the time. That's how I'd like to see her, as if that was how we first met, in the junior high classroom. Brought together through the quiet yet overpowering intercession of ammonites and coelacanths. Thinking this way about it makes all sorts of things easier to accept.

I was a healthy young fourteen-year-old boy, so much so that all it took was a warm west wind for my cock to snap to attention. That's the age I was. Not that she gave me an erection. She far surpassed any west wind. And not just the west wind. She was so spectacular that she made wind coming from *all* directions simply vanish. In the face of such an amazing girl how could I even think of having a sordid hard-on? It was first time in my life I'd met a girl who made me feel this way.

I have a sense that was the first time I met M. It didn't really happen that way, but thinking about it like this makes everything fall into place. I was fourteen, and she was fourteen too. That was the best age for us to have first encountered each other. That's how we really *should* have met.

But before I knew it, M was gone. Where to, I have no idea. One day, I lost sight of her. I happened to glance away for a moment, and when I turned back, she had disappeared. There one minute, gone the next. Some crafty sailor must have invited her to run off with him to Marseilles, or to the Ivory Coast. My despair was deeper than any ocean that they might have crossed. Deeper than any sea where giant squid and sea dragons swam. I started to hate myself. I couldn't believe in anything. How the hell had this happened? That's how much I loved M, how much she meant to me. How much I needed her. Why had I ever looked away?

Conversely, ever since then, M has been everywhere. I see her everywhere I go. She is part of many places, many times, many people. I put the half eraser in a plastic bag and carried it around with me like a talisman. Or a compass. As long it was in my pocket, I knew that someday, somewhere, I would find M again. I was sure of it. A smooth-talking sailor had sweet-talked her into boarding his big ship, and spirited her far away, that's all. She was always the type of girl who trusted others. The type who would take a brand-new eraser, break it in half, and offer it to a boy she didn't even know.

I tried to collect fragments of clues as to her where-abouts, in all sorts of places and from all sorts of people. But these were nothing but scraps, assorted bits and pieces. No matter how many you collect, fragments are still just that. Her essence always vanished like a mirage. And from land, the horizon was infinite. As was the horizon at sea. I busily chased it, moving from point to point—from Bombay to Cape Town to Reykjavik to the Bahamas. I made the rounds of every town with a harbor, but by the time I arrived, she was already gone. Only a faint trace of her warmth remained on an unmade bed. Her scarf with its whirlpool design lay hanging on the back of a chair. A half-read book, its pages open, on a table. Half-dry stockings hung out to dry in the bathroom. But she was no longer there. Cunning sail-ors around the world sensed me coming, and quickly snatched her away and hid her once more. By this time, of course, I'm no longer fourteen. I'm more suntanned, and tougher. My beard is thicker and I know the differ-ence between a metaphor and a simile. But a part of me is still fourteen. And the part of me that's forever fourteen waits, very patiently, for a gentle west wind to stroke my innocent penis. Wherever that west wind blows, M will surely be found.

That's M to me.

A woman who never stays in one place.

But not a woman who would take her own life.

I'm not exactly sure what I'm trying to say here. Maybe I'm trying to write about essence, rather than the truth. But writing about an essence that isn't true is like trying to rendezvous with someone on the dark side of the moon. It's dim and devoid of landmarks. And way too big. What I want to say is, M is the woman I should have fallen in love with when I was fourteen. But it was only much later that I fell in love with her, and by then, sadly, she was fourteen no more. We were mistaken about the time when we should have met. Like forgetting when you're supposed to meet someone. You get the time of day and place right, but miscalculate the day.

A fourteen-year-old girl still resided within her, however. That girl was complete inside of her, not just fragments. If I looked closely, I could catch a glimpse of that girl coming and going inside of M. When she lay in my arms as we made love, she would turn old one minute, then become a young girl in the next. She was always traveling in her own private time zone. And I loved her for that. I'd hold her tightly, so tightly that she said it hurt. I might have held her too hard. But I couldn't help it. I didn't want to give her up.

But, of course, the time came when I lost her again. All the sailors around the world, after all, had her in their sights. I couldn't be expected to protect her all by myself. No one can keep their eyes on someone every second. You have to sleep, have to use the bathroom. Need to scrub the bathtub sometime. Have to slice onions, have to snap off the ends of string beans. Check the air in the tires of your car. That's how we left each other. Or, rather, how she left me. There was always, in the background, the unambiguous shadow of a sailor. A single dark, autonomous shadow gliding up the wall of a building. Bathtubs, onions, and air were simply shards of metaphor scattered like thumbtacks by that shadow.

After she left, no one knows how wretched I felt, how deep the abyss. How could they? I can barely recall it myself. How much did I suffer? How much pain did I go through? I wish there was a machine that could accurately measure sadness, and display it in numbers that you could record. And it would be great if that machine could fit in the palm of your hand. I think of this every time I measure the air in my tires.

In the end, she died. The phone call in the middle of the night made that clear. I don't know where, or how, or why, or what the point was, but M decided to end her own life, and end it she did. And—probably—she then quietly withdrew from this real world. All the sailors in the world, and all their sweet talk, couldn't save her now—or even abduct her—from the land of the dead. But if you listen really closely in the middle of the night, maybe you, too, can catch the far-off sound of the sailors' mournful dirge.

When she died I lost my fourteen-year-old self. Like a baseball player's number that is permanently retired, the fourteen-year-old inside me up and left for good. My fourteen-year-old self was now locked away in a thick safe, intricately locked, buried on the bottom of the sea.

The door to the safe won't be opened for a billion years. Until then, ammonites and coelacanths will silently keep watch over it. The pleasant west wind no longer blows. And sailors all over the world mourn her passing. Not to mention all the anti-sailors around the world.

When I learned of M's death I felt sure I was the second-loneliest man on the planet.

The loneliest man had to be her husband. I reserve that seat for him. I have no idea what kind of person he is. I don't know how old he is. I have no information at all about what he does or doesn't do. The only thing I know is that he has a deep voice. But that doesn't tell me a thing. Is he a sailor? Or someone who opposes sailors? If the latter, that makes him one of my compatriots. If the former . . . I still feel for him. And I wish there was something I could do to ease his pain.

But there was no way I could find my former girl-friend's husband. I don't know his name, or the place where he lives. Perhaps he had already lost his name and place. He was, after all, the world's loneliest man. When I go on walks I like to sit down in front of the statue of a unicorn (the park with this particular unicorn statue is on my usual route), and as I gaze at the cold water in the fountain, I think about this man. And I imagine what it means to be the loneliest man on earth. I already know what it is to be the second-loneliest man on earth. But I still don't know what it is to be the loneliest. A deep gulf separates the second and the first loneliest on earth. Most likely. Deep, and wide, too. The bottom is heaped high with the corpses of birds who have tried, and failed, to traverse it.

Suddenly one day you become Men Without Women.

That day comes to you completely out of the blue, without the faintest of warnings or hints beforehand. No premonitions or foreboding, no knocks or clearing of throats. Turn a corner and you know you're already *there*. But by then there's no going back. Once you round that bend, that is the only world you can possibly inhabit. In that world you are called "Men Without Women." Always a relentlessly frigid plural.

Only Men Without Women can comprehend how painful, how heartbreaking, it is to become one. You lose that wonderful west wind. Fourteen is stolen away from you forever. (A billion years should count as forever.) The far-off, weary lament of the sailors. The bottom of the sea, with the ammonites and coelacanths. Calling someone's house past one a.m. Getting a call after one a.m. from a stranger. Waiting for someone you don't know somewhere between knowledge and ignorance. Tears falling on the dry road as you check the pressure of your tires.

As I sat there in front of the unicorn statue I prayed that someday her husband would recover. I prayed, too, that he would never forget the really important things—the *essence*—but would be able to forget everything else that was unimportant, and secondary. I hoped he could even forget the fact that he had forgotten them. I truly felt this way. Imagine that, I thought: here was the second-loneliest man on earth feeling compassion for—and praying for—the man who was the loneliest (someone he had never even met).

But why had he gone to the trouble of calling me? I'm not criticizing him for it, it's just that I can't answer this fundamental question, even now. How did he even know about me? And why did he care? The answer is probably simple. M must have told her husband about me. *Something* about me. That's the only thing I can imagine that make him call. *What* she told him, though, I have no idea. What value, what meaning, could I possibly have had for her, that she would tell her husband about a former boyfriend like me? Was it something critical connected to her death? Did I cast some sort of shadow over her passing? Maybe M told her husband how beautiful my penis is. When we lay in bed in the afternoon she used to lovingly hold it on her palm and gaze at it like she was admiring the legendary crown jewels of India. "It's sooo beautiful," she would say. Whether that's true or not, I have no clue.

Was this what made her husband call me? Phoning me up after one a.m. to express his respect for the shape of my cock? Hardly. That's absurd. Any way you look at it, my penis is less than spectacular. The best you could say is that it's pretty average. Her sense of beauty often left me shaking my head. She had an offbeat sense of values, unlike anyone else.

Probably (and I'm just imagining here) she told her husband about sharing half her eraser with me in the junior high classroom. She had no ulterior motive in telling him, and she meant well. It was just a small memory from the past that she happened to share. And of course this made him jealous. The fact that M gave me half of her eraser would have caused him to be much more jealous than if M had had sex with two busloads of sailors. It's only to be expected. What do two busloads of brawny sailors mean? M and I were, after all, both fourteen, and all it took for me to get an erection was the west wind.

Having a girl break her brand-new eraser in two and give me half was extraordinary. Like handing over a dozen old barns to a gigantic tornado.

After that, every time I pass the statue of the unicorn, I sit down there for a while and contemplate Men Without Women. Why that place? Why a unicorn? Maybe the unicorn, too, is one of the Men Without Women. I mean, I've never seen a unicorn couple. He—it has to be a *he*, right?—is always alone, sharp horn thrust toward the sky. Maybe we should adopt him as the symbol of Men Without Women, of the loneliness we carry as our burden. Perhaps we should sew unicorn badges on our breast pockets and hats, and quietly parade down streets all over the world. No music, no flags, no tickertape. Probably. (I'm using the word "probably" a bit too much. Probably.)

It's quite easy to become Men Without Women. You love a woman deeply, and then she goes off somewhere. That's all it takes. Most of the time (as I'm sure you're well aware) it's crafty sailors who take them away. They sweet-talk them into going with them, then carry them off to Marseilles or the Ivory Coast. And there's hardly anything we can do about it. Or else the women have nothing to do with sailors, and take their own lives. And there's very little we can do about that, too. Not even the sailors can do a thing.

In any case, that's how you become Men Without Women. Before you even know it. And once you've become Men Without Women, loneliness seeps deep down inside your body, like a red-wine stain on a pastel carpet. No matter how many home ec books you study, getting rid of that stain isn't easy. The stain might fade a bit over time, but it will still remain, as a stain, until the day you draw your final breath. It has the right to be a stain, the right to make the occasional, public, stain-like pronouncement. And you are left to live the rest of your life with the gradual spread of that color, with that ambiguous outline.

Sounds are different in that world. So is the way you experience thirst. And the way your beard grows. And the way baristas at Starbucks treat you. Clifford Brown's solos sound different, too. Subway-car doors close in new and unexpected ways. Walking from Omote Sando to Aoyama Itchome, you discover the distance is no longer what it once was. You might meet a new woman, but no matter how wonderful she may be (actually, the more wonderful she is, the more this holds true), from the instant you meet, you start thinking about losing her. The suggestive shadow of sailors, the sound of foreign tongues they speak (is it Greek? Estonian? Tagalog?), leaves you anxious. The names of exotic ports around the world unnerve you. Because you already know what it means to be Men Without Women. You are a pastel-colored Persian carpet, and loneliness is a Bordeaux wine stain that won't come out. Loneliness is brought over from France, the pain of the wound from the Middle East. For Men Without Women, the world is a vast, poignant mix, very much the far side of the moon.

M and I went out for about two years. Not a very long time. But a substantial two years. *Only* two years, you could say. Or a *long* two years. It all depends on your viewpoint. I say we "went out," but really we only saw each other two or three times a month. She had her reasons, and I had mine. At this point we were, unfortunately, no longer fourteen. And these reasons were what broke us apart. No matter how tightly I held on to her so she couldn't get away. And the thick, dark shadows of sailors still went on relentlessly, scattering sharp, metaphoric thumbtacks all around.

What I remember most about M is how much she loved elevator music. Percy Faith, Montovani, Raymond Lefèvre, Frank Chacksfield, Francis Lai, 101 Strings, Paul Mauriat, Billy Vaughan. She had a kind of predestined affection for this—according to me—harmless music. The angelic strings, the swell of luscious woodwinds, the muted brass, the harp softly stroking your heart. The charming melody that never faltered, the harmonies like candy melting in your mouth, the just-right echo effect in the recording.

I usually listened to rock or blues when I drove. Derek and the Dominos, Otis Redding, The Doors. But M would never let me play any of that. She always carried a paper bag filled with a dozen or so cassettes of elevator music, which she'd play one after the other. We'd drive around aimlessly while she'd quietly hum along to Francis Lai's "13 Jours en France." Her lovely, sexy lips with a light trace of lipstick. Anyway, she must have owned ten thousand tapes. And she knew all there was to know about all the innocent music in the world. If there were an Elevator Music Museum, she could have been the head curator.

It was the same when we had sex. She was always playing music in bed. I don't know how many times I heard Percy Faith's "A Summer Place" when we were doing it. It's a little embarrassing to say this, but even now I get pretty aroused whenever I hear that tune—my breathing ragged, my face flushed. You could scour the world and I bet you'd only find one man—me—who gets horny just hearing the intro to "A Summer Place." No—maybe her husband does too. Let's leave that possibility open. You could scour the world and probably find (including me) only two men who get all hot and bothered hearing the intro to "A Summer Place." Let's restate it this way. That'll work.

Space.

"The reason I like this kind of music," M said one time, "is a question of space."

"Space?"

"When I listen to this music I feel like I'm in a wide-open, empty place. It's a vast space, with nothing to close it off. No walls, no ceiling. I don't need to think, don't need to say anything, or do anything. Just being there is enough. I close my eyes and give myself up to the beautiful strings. There're no headaches, no sensitivity to cold, no periods, or ovulation. Everything is simply beautiful, peaceful, flowing. I can just *be*."

"Like you're in heaven?"

"Right," M said. "I'm sure in heaven Percy Faith is playing the background music. Would you rub my back some more?"

"Sure," I reply.

"You really give good back rubs."

Henry Mancini and I exchange a secret look, and a faint smile rises to our lips.

Elevator music is another item on the list of things I've lost. The thought hits me each time I go for a drive. While I'm waiting for the light to change, I half hope a girl I've never laid eyes on before will suddenly yank open the passenger door, slip inside, and, without a word or even a glance, jam a cassette with "A Summer Place" into the radio. I've even dreamed about it. Of course, it never happens. I mean, my car doesn't even have a cassette deck anymore. When I drive now, I use an iPod with a USB cable. And Francis Lai and 101 Strings are definitely not on my iPod. Gorillaz or the Black Eyed Peas are more like it.

That's what it's like to lose a woman. And at a certain time, losing one woman means losing all women. That's how we become Men Without Women. We lose Percy Faith, Francis Lai, and 101 Strings. And ammonites and coelacanths. And we lose her beautiful back. I used to rub M's back with my palm, in time to the soft triple beat of Henry Mancini's version of "Moon River." *Waiting round the bend, my Huckleberry friend . . .* But all of that has vanished. All that remains is an old broken piece of eraser, and the far-off sound of the sailors' dirge. And the unicorn beside the fountain, his lonely horn aimed at the sky.

I hope that M is in heaven now—or somewhere like it—enjoying "A Summer Place." Gently enveloped by that open, boundless music. I just hope there's no Jefferson Airplane playing. (Surely God wouldn't be that cruel.) And it would be nice if, as she listens to the pizzicato violins of "A Summer Place," her thoughts occasionally turn to me. But maybe that's asking too much. I pray that, even if I'm not part of it, M is happy and at peace, with Muzak playing on into eternity.

As one of the Men Without Women, I pray for this with all my heart. At this point prayer seems like the only thing I can do. Probably.

Translated by Philip Gabriel